ISBN 978-0-692-71549-9

http://www.writerashok.com

Infinite Love, Finite Life

A novella by

Ashok Thakur

Acknowledgements

I am grateful to Vishen Lakhiani of Mindvalley for giving me the framework to create this book and connecting me to the awesome human beings. Thank you to the following people for awakening the creativity of a left-brain dominated engineer and keeping my heart filled with their Love and Joy: Emily Fletcher of Ziva Meditation, Tony Award nominated Broadway and movie director Kristin Hanggi, as well as, actress and yoga instructor Natalie Roy. I also want to thank Jeannette Zeuner of Asaya Mind for her creative feedback during the final stages of the book, Prerna Thakur for her exceptional editing and proofreading talents, and all of my friends who have supported and inspired me throughout this process.

And finally, I give thanks to the Universe! These friends and mentors were sent to me by the Universe to guide throughout my awesome journey of growth both as an individual, and as a writer.

Dedication

To Prerna for being my shining star during the darkest period of my life and to Prateek for trusting me when I needed it most.

What is Love?

I wrote this book when all of my beliefs about Love were being challenged. I kept on writing and never read it completely, until it was finished. Only then did I realize that this book begins and ends with the word Love. I did not do this intentionally. I believe the Universe was showing me one simple truth- that we are Love. It is where we begin and it is where we end. Everything in between is a journey to understand that truth and enrich our souls in the process.

Chapter 1

Love is both complicated and simple. It is complicated if you think about it and simple if you feel it. Today, I felt so many emotions. I was not sure if I should cry or scream with joy. My body became nonphysical, with every part of it converted into a receptor of vibrations from the Universe. I am wiser now and understand the strange words that Nick used to say to me.

How can Ispi talk to me like that? He has no right to be so rude to me. He is not a teenager anymore. He has to understand my feelings and respect them. After what I did, to raise him and sacrifice my life for him, he should be more respectful. Today I am going to confront him and tell him all about his dad. Maybe that will make him understand my relationship with Mistico.

I still remember graduation day for Ispi. I was so happy that he completed his undergrad in Electrical Engineering. I rushed from the parking lot of his college to the graduation auditorium. All of a sudden, it became dark, there was loud thunder and it started raining heavily without any warning. I saw it caught few other parents by surprise too. I had nowhere to hide in the open parking lot. I was soaking wet. I was mad at myself. I should have brought an umbrella. I love rain, as it reminds me of my last days with Nick, when we were so much in love that it defies divinity. But not today, as his son was graduating and I was a mess before I reach graduation hall. My white blouse and black skirt were drenched. My black hair probably looked disgusting. I can't even imagine how messed up my makeup must have been. I was late for Ispi's graduation. It was very frustrating, the time and money I spent to get ready for his graduation wasted because of the rain. Suddenly I saw a young man running towards me with an umbrella. It seemed strange to me that he had an umbrella but he didn't think about opening it. He was soaking wet too. As he came closer, I was unable to recognize him. He wasn't one of Ispi's friends. When he approached, he lost his balance, slipped and fell on me. He was out of breath. He was running so fast as if he wanted to somehow rescue me from the torrential rain.

"Excuse me, I saw you from my dorm room and I rushed with an umbrella," he said as he opened the umbrella over my head. It was so windy that the umbrella flew away as soon as he opened it. He felt embarrassed and started running after it. He finally got hold of it and again tried to save me from getting wet. Then he realized that there were many holes in it.

"I'm so sorry. I didn't check the umbrella before heading out of my dorm. It hasn't rained yet this season, and I didn't realize it until now."

Then I really looked at him. He had brown curly hair somewhat in disarray and deep blue eyes. He was around Ispi's age, probably six feet tall, very muscular, with tanned skin. He was exceptionally handsome. He wore a t-shirt, jeans and flip-flops. As soon as our eyes met, I felt a strange emotion that sent shivers through my whole body. I hadn't felt like that for many years. Actually I can't remember ever feeling like that before. I guess since Nick died, I was almost dead for feeling anything.

I thought I was struck by lightning. It was like my whole body was made of Aloe Vera gel—transparent and gooey. I felt his thoughts passing through my clear body and touching right in my heart and it made me very uncomfortable. I thought he was probably a friend of Ispi and simply saw his friend's mom needed help.

"Who are you?" I asked. "Do I know you? And why did you come running so fast? I'm okay. You didn't have to….rescue me." I nearly choked on those final words.

"I'm Mistico. I know you very well and I came to help you. It is a payback for all you did for me. I'm sorry I had to go back then, but I am here now."

I had no idea what he meant. I seriously thought he was probably smoking marijuana and needed to come to his senses.

"I don't know what you're talking about. You must be confusing me with someone else," I said as we started moving towards the graduation hall. "I am here for my son Ispi's graduation."

"No, I am not confusing you with anyone else. I know it is you and I have been waiting for you for years." He was very assertive and sure. He told me he was completing a master's in Music Performance and had one more year to finish his thesis.

"What is…your subject…for thesis?" I tried to keep the conversation alive as we ran in the heavy rain.

"Past life…regression…through music," he murmured.

As we talked, I started to feel very comfortable with him. Strangely comfortable. He told me he was playing the saxophone at the graduation ceremony and he almost forgot about it. He suddenly turned and ran back to his dorm, leaving his umbrella with me. I stood there perplexed as he disappeared in the torrential rain. It happened so fast. I had to pinch myself to confirm the whole thing was real.

I thought it was a dream and held myself together. I started walking towards the lobby. A pretty young girl with red hair and hazel eyes wearing black skirt came up to me. I must have looked like one hell of a mess. She approached me directly and asked if I need help.

"I could use some dry clothes," I said jokingly, but she was serious.

"Hi, I'm Mandy. I saw Mad Mistico just left you and ran away."

"Do you know him?" I asked.

"Yes."

"Are you his girlfriend?"

"Not really. I play flute with him in his band. No one knows him well. He seems very distant. He's always looking for something, staring into a vacuum, as if he lost his most precious thing and had trouble finding it. He is a great musician though. When he plays solo, it touches your heart and takes you to a very peaceful place in a faraway land. Everyone says that, not just me. It feels like your life is lifted from chaos to ultimate serenity. It's as if your soul is filled with love…" She trailed off, lost in her thoughts.

I looked outside. The rain had stopped but it had done the damage. She offered me to come to her dorm and borrow her clothes.

"But… Sorry, what's your name?"

"Mandy."

"Thanks Mandy, but I'll be late for graduation."

"No, you won't be. They are trying to fix some electrical issue from the thunderstorm. They just announced, it will start an hour late."

I agreed to go with Mandy. I changed my clothes and dried my hair. Her clothes fit me correctly except they were little tight and showed a lot of cleavage, partially due to the fact that I had a lot of cleavage to show. As if she read my thoughts, she then gave me a beautiful, colorful scarf with flowers and butterflies all over it. I was a little uncomfortable but I didn't have any other choice. The graduation ceremony was about to begin. Mandy left me and made her way behind the stage. I sat on the right side of the auditorium. I had no idea why she had gone out of her way to help me, but somehow I felt very close to her.

The ceremony started and there he was, playing his tenor. He was playing in the band with other musicians but my eyes were focused on him. It was as if my internal body camera had a zoom just on him. I was very upset with myself for having such strange emotions.

After the ceremony, Ispi came to me. He was angry that I had embarrassed him in front of his friends, wearing such tight clothes and showing cleavage. He didn't believe me when I told him the whole story.

"Mom, firstly you are dressed like a …. And then you are making up some silly story to cover your craziness."

I told him that I had to return these clothes to Mandy who lives in the dorm right next to the building.

"Mom, there is no dorm next to the building. Stop making up funny stories. You are always weird, talking about mystic shit. The fact is there is no Mandy. You created it in your imagination to justify your stupid idea of dressing like a stripper."

I knew I should have never told him about my past life. He kept using it to belittle me. I didn't know when he would understand and stop judging me for the things that happened in the past. Ispi said he had to go to an after party at a dance club and left. I felt so depressed with his behavior, I wanted to cry. I didn't have a crying shoulder since Nick passed away. I always pretended to be tough as I had to raise my son alone. I didn't want him to feel the absence of his dad. In fact, I had been very lonely and sad for many years.

I got hold of my emotions and started looking for Mandy's dorm. At first, I thought I was lost as there was no dorm just outside the building. I took a long stroll all around and was unable to find Mandy's dorm. This campus always confused me. I lost my sense of direction or may be Ispi was right. Did I create it in my imagination? But what about her clothes? They were real and she knew Mistico. I was not going crazy after all. Was I?

I started walking back to my car feeling very disturbed by my son's behavior. As I was approaching my car, Mistico appeared from nowhere. Maybe I was so deep in my thoughts, I didn't see him coming.

"Did you think I would let you get away with my royal umbrella?" he joked.

I didn't know how to react to his comment. I was kind of shocked. Where did he come from?

"What is your name?" he asked.

"Veronica." I didn't want to say it but it popped out from my subconscious.

"I am going to be playing the sax at an after party. Will you join me?"

I was amazed by his blunt question. He was talking to me as if he had known me forever. "I'm sorry but I am too old for late night parties."

"Fine, then I won't go to the party either. There is a nice coffee shop outside the campus. Let's go there and have coffee. You have no idea how long I have been waiting for this day."

"I don't drink coffee," I said, trying to avoid him and moving towards my car.

"But can you spend some time with me?" He was so persistent. It made me little uncomfortable.

"Isn't playing at the after party important to you?"

"It is," he said, "but spending time with you is more important."

His voice and expressions changed from asking to insist. Something inside me told me I couldn't ignore him anymore. I told him I would go to the place where he is playing but I was not going to stay long. He was happy. Really happy, like a little kid who had gotten the best toy in the world. He held my hand and walked with me to his car. I felt a rush of adrenalin by his touch. It was like I was thirteen again and had been touched by a boy for the first time. I was very confused and trying to process my insane emotions. I could hear his heart thumping loudly. Or was it my heart? I didn't know I was still capable of having these kinds of emotions. I almost forgot that we were going somewhere. Time had stopped. Blood rushed through whole body like a flood. I thought my veins were going to explode. The dormant hormones probably woke up to the call of inevitable love.

We stood in the parking lot holding hands. The spectrum of light from the lamp post behind him made him look like a giant boy with big shoulders. He had this weird fedora on his head that made him look like character from an old noir film. As if he read my mind, he took off his fedora. He looked like a movie star and I was totally ecstatic. I even forgot I was much older than him and fell completely in love. I didn't feel like leaving his hand to sit in the car. He probably felt the same. We stood there for a long time and stared into each other's eyes without saying a word. Silence never felt that comfortable. As if we had nothing to say, as if we were long lost friends but knew everything about each other.

We didn't say anything while driving. I had a strange feeling sitting on the passenger seat right next to him. It felt like I was light as a feather, relaxed and calm. It was as if my body lost all its weight and I was floating on clouds.

Chapter 2

He parked in the club parking lot and went to the passenger side to open the door for me. As I climbed in, his hand touched my breasts. I looked up at his face and shivered under his hard touch. I felt so sexy, I wanted to kiss him right there and then. My social programming was able to stop me. I'm sure he felt the same way as he quivered and unhooked his eyes from mine. I felt guilty about the whole thing and didn't say a word till we were in the club.

He made me sit at a corner table and ordered a drink for me, then he excused himself to go play at the little podium. Mistico started playing with the band. He was playing Santana's "Black Magic Woman". It was very loud and crazy in the club. Everyone was knocking back shots and having fun. I felt completely out of place there.

Our server came and asked if I want another round, and I started to chat with her a little. I asked about Mistico and she melted. Her nametag said "Kim". Kim told me he plays in the club every Friday and Saturday. She asked him to go out after work many times but he doesn't pay any attention to her or any other girls. I thought he was waiting for someone special that may never happen.

"He's playing very intuitively tonight with a lot more passion than usual. He also looked at me and smiled, which is rare. Something must have changed in his life today. He doesn't have that lost look in his eyes," she said.

She asked, "How do you know him?"

I didn't know how to answer that.

"He is a friend," I said reluctantly.

Kim looked at me with a surprise and told me that I should come here more often. She would love to have deeper conversation with me. She asked if she could have my contact information. I reluctantly gave her my phone number and told her I'd come back.

It was late and I wanted to go home but something inside me made me stay. After he was done playing, he came to me and told me it was his best performance so far. He felt that the music came from his heart. He didn't have to think what to play. It was magical.

He dropped me back off at the campus parking lot.

"When can I see you again?"

"Why?" I asked.

"Because I love you and I miss you!" I could see tears in his eyes.

I stepped out from the passenger seat. "How can you miss me? We just met today." I must admit, I was feeling the same way but was reluctant to say it. "What kind of a love is this?" I asked him. "Are you saying you love me in a romantic way?"

"Of course, yes," he asserted.

"You realize I am much older than you and we probably don't have similar interests or backgrounds, right? You should be going out with someone your age."

"But I have been waiting for you for years and I want to be with you."

What I was saying had nothing to do with what I was thinking. I felt good that a young, handsome and sexy guy was paying so much attention to me. It appealed to my ego. I felt wetness in my thighs and starting to crumble on my feet. He held me in his muscular arms and put me in the back seat of my SUV. He grabbed the water bottle from the front and gave it to me. I was gasping for breath. A strange feeling of ecstasy spread through my whole body. He slid inside the car from the other side and held my head in his lap. I could feel he was getting hard and uncomfortable but he didn't want to leave. He turned to me and started kissing me on my neck, behind the ear and then on random parts of my body. I was feeling so hot and sexy. I laid there pretending I was not. Then he started moving his hand all over my body, caressing with his fingertips around my breasts, on my thighs, behind my back. He moved my wandering curly hair from my face. He lifted me up from the seat and slid me gently in his lap with my hardened nipples touching against his muscular chest. He gently took my top off, slipped my breasts out of the bra and started kissing my nipples with his sensuous lips. That kissing changed to gentle sucking and I felt so connected to him. He started kissing me on my lips, and the love juices overflowed in my body.

At this point, I was unable to resist the temptation. He took off his shirt. I glanced outside in the parking lot. It was pitch dark and raining lightly. Suddenly there was a streak of lightning and his whole body was bathed in a striking blue color. My heart overtook my logical thoughts and I slid my hand in his pants. We made love so deeply that my whole body was shivering and melting in a bliss. It was so intense that I thought something in my body was going to come out and I was going to die right there.

We stayed there a long time after and didn't say a thing. It was early morning and clouds waned away. Moonlight filtered through the windows. It was serene and mystic. We exchanged phone numbers and reluctantly separated from each other. I always wondered how people make love in the back seat as it must be very uncomfortable. Now I know that when you are in love, many of your senses shut down and you only feel the goodness.

Chapter 3

I was always stressed after Ispi was born. I had to raise Ispi as a single mother and he wasn't the easiest child to raise. He had too many questions about his dad. He was very critical and judgmental. He was upset when he realized that I had to work in a strip club as a dancer. He was upset about his dad, who he had never met.

Mistico and I started meeting at my apartment. I got weird looks from my neighbors as he started visiting me more frequently. I had such a great time. We made passionate love night after night. We must have been very loud. Even the Russian lady downstairs who never speaks with anyone due to lack of her conversational skills, got out of her comfort zone and confronted me.

My sister, who I see almost once a month, noticed that I was getting younger in my looks, behavior and feelings. I told her about Mistico and she had gone quiet for almost fifteen minutes to understand what it meant. She thought I was going insane and didn't understand what I was doing.

"What do you think your nieces and nephew will think. He is probably younger than my son. How did you even get the idea that it is alright to get into a relationship like that?"

"But we love each other," I told her.

"That is the most ridiculous thing I have heard from a grown woman. You are acting like a teenager. For God's sake, stop all this nonsense now."

I ignored her grudging tone and told her I would think about it, but I knew in my heart that nothing was going to change how I feel about him.

Mistico and I became the best friends and lovers as the time passed. We danced in the rain and played in the snow. We hung out together every weekend in strange places and went to exotic parties where people were not critical about our relationship. We got drunk together and ate at restaurants, smoked in lounges and on the street corners. We laid on the beach smoking marijuana. We made love under the full moonlight reflecting on the ocean water. We walked endlessly, hugging and kissing in the dark nights on the vagabond roads. We had the best time of our lives.

I lost a lot of friends and family as they were not happy with our relationship. We also made new friends who were not judgmental, who understood that you fall in love with a soul and not a body. We drove through the Rocky Mountains of Arizona and spent weeks on Indian reservations. We woke up in each other's arms every day and watched the golden sunrise and laid on a broken love seat on the deck staring at the beautiful sunset in the Canyons. We talked with the cactus plants in the dark, starry nights. What a life we had! We looked at the stars in the clear sky lying quietly in the deserts. We made love on the top of the mountains and in rainforests. We bathed in the most beautiful falls and hot springs. We felt that the Universe was aligned completely in our favor and would manifest whatever our wishes and desires were.

Years passed and our love blossomed with every sunrise and sunset, with every season. We loved life so much that I started questioning if it was real or a dream. How long could this possibly go on for? That's when my attention focused on the first gray hair on my head, the first wrinkle on my face, first pain in my back and knees. I realized that I was getting old and he was still in the prime of his youth. I couldn't be selfish and expect him to stay with me forever. It is not fair. A feeling of guilt crept over me. I started sabotaging the amazing love we shared.

Guilt and doubts are the biggest enemies for us and the people we love. As soon as we let them seep into our minds, they start eating us like a termite from inside, without us even knowing about it. They multiply, bringing in more negative emotions and more guilt, destroying us completely. If we want to enjoy life the way the Universe means us to, we have to keep these toxic killers of guilt, doubt and judgment out of our lives forever. Then and only then, we can achieve feelings of ecstasy, love and fulfillment together.

I started pushing him away from me, as I thought that was best for him. We have to stop being self-sacrificing for the sake of others we love so dearly. We have to stop making decisions about their lives and steering them the way we think is good. Who are we to decide what is good for someone? We have to stop being protective and let them stumble and fall and learn their own lessons. We need to surrender to the beauty and grandeur of the Universe. Souls know how to evolve themselves. It is when we start messing with the natural flow of being that we block the ultimate joy of life. That's exactly what I started doing to our amazing love.

We rented a hut deep in the Amazon to spend more time with nature away from everything and everyone. Being alone in the woods, away from all distractions, I started thinking about our beautiful life and pondering our future together.

"Mistico, I think I am getting too old for all this excitement and crazy lifestyle."

"What do you mean?" he said, perplexed as if he doesn't understand a word I said.

"I am not going to be around to share life with you for a long time. You should be seeing others." It was so weird to hear myself say these words, as if even I wasn't convinced about what I was saying. It didn't seem to be coming from me.

"What is going on, darling? Are you okay? Is something bothering you?"

"Well… Obviously I am much older than you and it is a fact that I am going to die well before you. I want you to be with someone your age so she can be with you for the rest of your life. I will help you to find a nice girlfriend." The words sounded so foreign and strange to me, my voice started cracking and my eyes welled with tears.

I saw tears in his eyes too, as if I hurt his deepest feelings. He didn't say a word and just stood and walked into the woods. I wanted him to have some quiet time to think about it.

It started raining heavily. The jungle takes a life of its own and creates a different personality altogether with different sounds and noises. I felt like I was in a Disney movie, only it was real and not enhanced by IMAX special effects.

It continued raining torrentially as if the clouds had ripped open. He didn't come back yet. I ate some fruits and fell asleep. I was woken up by the golden rays of morning sun seeping into the wooden cabin. I went out thinking he must have come back and would be sitting outside on the bench. He wasn't there. I didn't think much of it. Sometimes when he gets up early, he goes for a walk through the jungle to the river. He takes a shattered raft that is there on the banks and floats across the river to the falls. He told me that I look like a baby when I am sleeping in the morning with rays of sun playing with my curly hairs dancing on my cheeks with wind and it would be sinful to wake me up. I often thought he puts me on a pedestal to worship like a goddess. I get scared sometimes just thinking about it. I am not that special. Why does he give me so much love? Am I worthy of it?

The day ended quickly and he wasn't back. Days turned into weeks and weeks turned into months. Every passing moment made me more anxious and fearful. I waited and waited with no sign of him, with every drop of rain, every ray of morning sun, every sunset, every phase of the moon, every whisper of wind, every sound of crickets, every rumbling of clouds and thunder, I got new hope. Every morning I woke up to be with him again and then every night I slept alone. My heart wept, my eyes like stone on the broken wooden steps. I had no hunger, no sleep, just a hope that he would return.

I have been waiting for twelve years. Nobody knows what happened to him. Am I going to see him again in this life? In the same body or a different one? Maybe my soul has to leave this body and meet him in some other world. I don't know. Why does such a pure love have to suffer? I am starting to get weak, physically and mentally. The local Shaman came this morning to see me. He told me that I am very sad inside and have to let go. I don't know what it means. How can I let him go without saying goodbye, without a promise to meet again soon, without a final kiss, without a cuddle, without running my fingers through his hairs, without looking into his deep blue eyes? I am still waiting and have no idea when this wait is going to be over.

If he is a soul, why doesn't he give me some signal that he is all right? Probably all those questions are going to die with me. I am still waiting for my eternal and infinite Love in this finite life.

I love and I hug as I am alive

I laugh and I cry as I am alive

I kiss and I miss as I am alive

I fall and I rise as I am alive

My wounded heart is open so love can flow

My eyes are wide open to see your glow

I fall in the puddles

To get your cuddles

Come to me, my love, so we can snuggle

Chapter 4

This is not my story. It is his story. Nick is no more. I don't know how to write anything. I never wrote anything, not even a few lines in a journal. His story needs to be told so I am writing this for me and not for anyone else. My writing skills are not good, but I am hoping my emotions and thoughts for Nick somehow manifest into the physical world of realty and recreate his beautiful life on paper. It will provide insight into how a human being can rise above the mundane and can inspire someone to live their life to the fullest. His love was for everyone, for all who came in touch with him in this journey of his soul. We probably cannot think how someone with that much zest towards life can be alone when he dies. He was alone, but not lonely, as he feels the infinite love that he shared with me and everyone around him. He told me, "Sweetheart, when I go, there will be no one around me, absolutely no one, as I will not have any money, no estate, and no kids to light my fire."

"I will be there with you, Nick," I said.

He didn't answer. Either he wasn't convinced or he knew already. He could see future events as he told me exactly when we met for the first time. He told me that one day I would understand why he loves me so much. It sounded weird and unconventional to me. He would talk with so much passion about everything and with everyone from janitors, waiters, receptionists, the rich, the poor, homeless, to garage attendants. He saw the goodness in everyone and spread his love all around.

I asked, "Nick, how come everyone is good in your opinion? There are people who are definitely bad."

"Sweetie, they are just good human beings whose goodness was turned negative due to an incident, event or thought. We have to turn them upside-down and the goodness will come pouring out again. They will start shining and speaking the language of Love." He laughed and said jokingly, "That's why I love yoga, so I can stand upside-down on my head."

"You mean to say my ex-boyfriend who was a total asshole by any measure, is a good guy too?" I disagreed and laughed back.

But he didn't laugh. He was serious.

His expression changed to calm and glowing. I noticed this before when he talked of the spiritual and mystic stuff; it felt like he transformed into someone else who had transcended into a different time-space reality and started telling me his complex theory of soul evolution that was beyond my comprehension anyway.

"The challenge is not to be compassionate and forgive everyone who has hurt you or is trying to destroy you with physical and mental pain. That part is simple. The tough and more gracious thing is to still Love them when they are hurting you. They are the souls on their own journey and they are just fulfilling their divine purpose. Their job is to teach you some lessons. Everyone is doing the job assigned to them by the Universe. So why hate anyone for doing their job?"

I didn't know how a casual conversation about my ex could end up being so serious.

Chapter 5

It was a routine day, boring and slow. I was waiting for my shift to be over so I could go home. I was working as a part-time waitress in the food court at the airport when I first saw him. He wore a button-down blue shirt, light mustard-color casual pants, and Lacoste shoes. He had deep blue eyes and straight black uncombed hair gave him an unconcerned, casual look. He walked into the place like he didn't have a worry in life. His eyes had a special glow and something in his personality had a magnetic pull. I didn't know what that attraction was, but I hoped he would sit at one of my tables. He did, totally unaware of my presence. I walked to his table to take his order. I never knew that this moment would change my life forever. For the first time in my life, I could feel vibrations in my body when I approached him. I felt weak walking towards him, but I shrugged it off as nothing at first. Girls my age generally feel that way when they see a hot-cool guy. He didn't fit into that mold though. He wasn't hot and was old for me.

"Hi, my name is Veronica. I will be your server today. Do you want something to drink?" I somehow mustered the courage to ask.

"I will take a Corona with lime," he said.

When I came back with the beer, he asked me my name again as if making sure.

He said, "You are a very good soul and I feel a strange connection to you. May I have your phone number?" He paused, but only briefly. "Sorry, I know I am being forward. But I would like to have dinner with you and get to know you better."

That literally creeped me out. I was a stunning girl by any standards and I was used to guys using pickup lines before, but this was somehow different. Subtle, but with a kind of intensity.

I couldn't say no and promised him that when he is done with his dinner, I will give him my number.

He said, "Let us not wait until the end of dinner. I know you will not be able to give me the phone number later."

I just smiled and went back to work. I thought about him while he was eating dinner. I wanted to know more about him. I even wrote my phone number on a dinner napkin. I would give it to him with his bill.

BANG!

The noise shook the restaurant. People were terrified and running around like crazy, screaming and yelling. I couldn't understand what was going on. I was so deep in thought trying to figure out his next move that I didn't realize a plane had missed the runway and slammed into the food court. Debris and smoke filled the dining room. Flames curled into the air. People were hurt. Airport security evacuated the whole place. I felt a sudden pain, then everything went black.

When I regained consciousness, my first thought was that he could have been a terrorist. How else could he have predicted that I wouldn't be able to give him my phone number? I began asking questions and found out that the investigators determined the accident was due to a pilot error.

Years later when I knew him better, I asked, "Nick, how did you know I would not be able to give you my number?"

"Because I saw this happen before," he said.

"What do you mean?" I asked. "It happened earlier with you and another girl?"

"No. It happened with you and me. I was searching for you since then."

"Are you crazy? When? We had just met."

"But I knew your soul. It happened to us in our past life."

"But there were no cell phones back then." I laughed. "How could you ask for my phone number?"

Time passed and my life changed. I had financial needs that my waitress salary could not fulfill. I started working as an exotic dancer in a club. The money was good, but there was a vacuum in my heart. Sometimes when I was tired and lonely after a night of work, I thought about him. I didn't even know his name.

Sometimes I thought about going to all the hospitals where they took injured people from the accident to find out about him, but I had nothing to go on.

More so, my mind convinced me that it would result in nothing as I had no name, no pictures, no address, and no phone number.

Chapter 6

One Monday night, it was my day off and I had the TV on while nuking leftover Chinese food when I heard on the news that one of the patients that was injured in the accident had gained consciousness after a six-year coma. They were showing his picture. It was him. He seemed much weaker, but I could recognize him nonetheless.

I put on my jacket and rushed to the hospital. I told them I was his friend. They started asking me about who he is. During the fire and chaos at the airport, many people lost their wallets. They were able to find relatives for all of them but Nick. He was in a coma and they had no knowledge of who he was and were unable to find his family. He still doesn't remember anything. Strangely, the only thing he remembers is the accident and he was asking for a girl who worked at the burger place in the food court. That sent a chill up my spine. How is it possible that he has forgotten all of his life's memories but remembers me who he met for only a few minutes?

I told them that I had no information about him, but demanded to see him.

There he was lying on the bed, lifeless, staring blankly at the door. I had changed my looks a lot during these years. I didn't think anyone who met me only once, six years ago, could even recognize me even if I told them who I was. As soon as he saw me, his eyes lit up. My whole body started vibrating with a strange feeling. I felt my heart beating very fast.

He said, "Here is my mystery girl and this time you are not leaving without giving me your number."

The nurse and doctor who accompanied me were surprised beyond belief. They say it was a miracle and beyond the comprehension of medical science. They started asking him his name and address. That is when I came to know that his name is Nick, but he couldn't remember anything else. The doctor said he needed rest and some kind of an injection to help him sleep.

Nick screamed, "Not before I get the phone number of my soul mate."

No, I knew I wasn't his soul mate, I couldn't be. He is twice my age, how is that possible? Also he probably had a family somewhere with a wife, kids, brothers, sisters, a mother and father. His wife is his soul mate, not me… But I gave him my number anyway and promised him I would come again to see him.

A few years later when I asked him about that incident, he told me that we often confuse our partners in life as soul mates.

I started visiting him in the hospital more often as doctors told me that it may help to bring his memory back. However, his memory didn't come back; the only person he remembered before the accident was me. There was a possibility that I could help him to gain back his memory and link to his past. The doctors wanted to discharge him in my care. My job was paying me handsomely, but I was not emotionally prepared for this. However I felt morally obligated to him. How can I leave someone who trusted me so much? I took him home temporarily until he recovered from memory lapses and figured out who he is and where his family is. My sister and mom thought I was crazy. They didn't want me to carry this emotional baggage. They wanted me to fall in love with a man of my age, get married and settle down.

Nicks says that souls seek each other and find the ones they are looking for without any boundaries of life and death. It so happened that one day, I met this girl Natasha in the supermarket and we became good friends instantly. She came to our house for a pool party on Memorial Day and met Nick. They started a conversation while I was taking care of other guests and she told me that Nick is from Italy. I was surprised and asked her how she knows. Natasha, being half Italian, started talking to him and he had a whole conversation with her in fluent Italian.

I asked Natasha what else he had said.

She told me that all he knows is that he is here to be with his soul mate that he lost in his past life.

That night Nick told me that he remembered he is from Rome and he has a wife, a daughter and a son. I was so happy for him. He started remembering everything, his address, his family, but couldn't recall his phone number. I finally found his home phone number and called his wife. I wanted to make sure before I put him on a flight to Italy, that there would be someone there to receive him. She answered and told me that I had the wrong number and she didn't know what I was talking about. I tried to do some more research and found that Nick had a successful export business in Rome that was sold by his wife five years earlier. When I asked Nick about it, he confirmed that he'd had a flourishing business. He had been on a business trip when he met me at the airport that day.

Nick wondered why no one came looking for him. Later, we came to find out that his wife had known where he was, but chose to ignore it and marry her boyfriend. She convinced the kids that their Dad had a girlfriend in America and had abandoned the whole family for her. So his whole family hated him and didn't want to even talk about him.

Chapter 7

Nick left for Italy. He wanted to go back to his family. He wanted to find out what happened to them. What are they doing? What is happening in their lives?

I got a strange sinking feeling when I dropped him off at the airport. He told me he felt a strong connection with me that can't be separated by anything, anymore. He said he would be back soon to see me. I think with all this time spent together he started to grow on me. I may be in love with him, but I am not sure it makes any sense. I am totally confused and don't know how to express these feelings. Maybe souls do travel through lifetimes and I am his lost soul mate from a past life? There are a lot more questions than answers. I shut off my mind and try to forget everything.

Months pass by and then months turn into years. Still no word from Nick. Sometimes I wonder what happened to him. How come he never called? What happened to our deepest connection at the soul level? I shrugged off these thoughts by taking shelter behind my logical thinking. He's probably been living happily with his family in Italy while I am here alone, still thinking about him.

I tried, but was unable to fall in love with anyone else and move on. I would compare everyone with Nick and try to find the love he had for me. I was the happiest person when I was with him for the shortest amount of time. He had a spark in his eyes whenever he looked at me. It feels like there were a thousand alive spirits that brought a shine to his eyes and brightened my days.

Life has moved on and I tried to adjust to the routine. I was making lot of money working as an exotic dancer. It was very exciting for my clients, my mom and sister, but dull for me. I needed to make a change in my life. Natasha told me that a spiritual teacher is going to hold a seminar in the city about awakening your sixth sense. She wanted to go, but needed company. I was so bored and depressed that I decided to go. The seminar opened up my heart to the infinite possibilities and completely changed my way of thinking. I started feeling the emotions rather than having the emotions come and go through me with no purpose. That's when I realized that all this time I was in love with Nick. So, I am going to Italy to see him. The urge was so intense that I grabbed my passport, bought a ticket and flew to Rome the next week.

It was a beautiful June day in Rome. I felt the pleasant air touching my skin and blowing my hair. I never felt so good in my life. It felt like I was a new person and closer to my destiny. I could feel the vibrations and my heart was beating so fast that I could feel it in my chest. I had never been to Rome, but it definitely felt like the best city in the world to me. There were celebrations all around for Festa della Repubblica, the national holiday that commemorates Italy becoming a republic. I realized even though I hadn't eaten for many hours, I was not hungry. It was as if some energy drove me towards a strange unknown destination. Just the thought of meeting Nick again took over all my body functions. I wasn't hungry, tired or sleepy at all. I knew I loved Nick, but I was never truly in love with him. I didn't know how it feels to be in love. I wanted to hold onto that feeling and capture it forever. I was afraid if that feeling was going to last and I didn't want to lose it. It felt so good, indescribable beyond words.

It is like asking a blind person to describe the colors of a sunset. Only someone who is truly in love can know that feeling and lucky are the souls that fall in love. It gives you a sense of purpose, a feeling of being alive, inspired and in spirit. The feeling permeates and oozes out of you. Everyone who is around you, even strangers will know that something divine is happening to you. You will stop caring about the mundane and will have love for everyone.

It is strange that our hearts can only hold one feeling at a time. If you love someone, you will be unable to hold hate for anyone. Before today, I hated Nick's ex-wife for abandoning him in America. Now I don't feel that anymore. I am not sure if I can ever forget how she treated him, but who knows? Love is so strange that it can do miracles. It can let you believe in Magic. I will hold onto that feeling even if I think it is not real. I wish I could have better words to describe it so you can feel what I felt that day. Still, I know you will somehow get the feeling and understand just by reading this if you do it with an open heart.

How could I be in love with a man twenty years older than me and didn't even express his love for me? There was no future in this relationship, but my heart would stop at nothing and want to move on without reason. Hearts stop listening to the mind and deny any idea that is not congruent with Love. That is why none of the love stories make sense to us. They are to be understood by the heart. That is why Lovers looks insane, because sanity is defined by the mind and Love is felt by the heart!

I started my search for Nick. I realized I was doing things that would seem insane. Emotions took over me and my brain stopped thinking. I wanted to check in to my hotel first, but instead I took a cab to the only address I knew in Italy—Nick's home.

A beautiful girl probably around eight years old opened the door.

I asked, "Does Nick live here, honey?"

She called her mom and said there is woman at the door asking for someone. That gave me a sinking feeling for a moment that I would not be able to find Nick after coming all this way.

A woman around my age with silky black hair and big beautiful eyes came to the door. She was incredibly beautiful. I am not sure what state of mind I was in, but everyone and everything looked very beautiful to me as if I got new eyes directly connected to my heart with no attachment to my brain.

She asked politely, "Who are you and what are you looking for?"

"I am not sure, but I was looking for Nick who used to live here many years ago."

I told her that I am Veronica and I came from America looking for Nick. I saw her beautiful face immediately turn into a tense frown.

She angrily said, "He doesn't live here anymore."

"Do you have a forwarding address or do you know anyone who can help me find him?" I asked.

She looked very upset with the conversation. She told her daughter to go inside. I thought she was going to explode with anxiety as she said, trying to control her emotions, "I am his daughter and you are the inconsiderate American bitch who ruined our family."

I would have argued with her to prove my innocence, but I didn't even care at that point. "Do you know where can I find him?" I asked.

"Probably in a homeless shelter or prison somewhere," she said with disgust.

I couldn't understand why she had so much hate for him. Now the Leo in me was more determined to find him. After weeks of searching all the homeless shelters in Rome, I was getting ready to go back to America. I got a message from my sister, Maria, saying that Nick was at our house, in the States, asking for me. A feeling of euphoria took over me. I was unable to contain my excitement. I took the next flight home. That was the longest journey. It felt like the flight took a trip around the globe before it finally landed. Maria came to pick me up at the airport, but Nick wasn't there with her. I was shocked. After all I had gone through to find him, he didn't even come to the airport. How rude!

Maria told me that he got very sick that morning and they took him to the hospital. I told her to drive straight to the hospital. That is where I met him again after a long time. He looked so different, I wouldn't have recognized him if I had seen him on the street. We were so happy to see each other. I asked him a million questions like what was going on in all these years, and why didn't he contact me. He smiled and said he would tell me everything when we got home.

Chapter 8

This is Nick's journal that he left for me and asked me not to read before he died. I guess he didn't want me to know how much effort he had put into seeing me after he was released from jail.

<u>Journey of Life</u>

This is my first day out of jail. I feel free and it seemed to be the brightest day I have ever seen. The Sun was shining brightly. I wasn't expecting anyone to pick me up, but strangely Michael was there. I knew him for years, but never realized that he would be so concerned about me. I probably see him once or twice a year at business parties. When I saw him today, I was overwhelmed with emotion. I never knew how much he loved me and was waiting to see me. He wanted to fill me in on what went on with my wife and kids after I was gone. He was filled with anger and rage towards my wife.

He was furious as he started speaking. "How can she falsely accuse you of all these things that you never did? I don't know why one human being could do such a horrendous act to another. Why did God let her do all this and get away with it? I hired a great lawyer to fight this case and teach her a lesson. We can't let her get away with this."

It felt like he was more upset and rancorous with her than I was. Just the thought of her atrocious acts were making him vengeful. His face turned red and I could see his twitching eyes and sinking frown.

"What does it matter now? I was already prosecuted for the crimes I didn't commit. I am not going to get those years back. I want to move on with my life."

"But Nick, you can't let her get away with it. You have to clear your name, at least for your kids who think you are such a bad person that they don't even want to see you. She has filled their hearts with so much venom that they didn't even come to see you in jail," he protested.

He took me to his home. His wife, Anna, had already prepared the guestroom for me. We ate lunch and I slept for hours. I was feeling much relaxed. I took a shower and we sat down on the dinner table. Anna started asking me questions about me and my wife to ease the razor-sharp silence that was somehow creeping on the dining table. I was so sad, I didn't want to talk about her.

"Nick, you have to get over it. It looks like you are still in love with her. You have to move on with your life," she grunted.

"How can I be in love with her after what she did to me? And what life should I move on to? I didn't know any life existed other than with her. I don't have any idea where to start. I am frozen in this phase of life. I don't know if I ever get out of it and how," I replied reluctantly.

I started feeling more depressed. Michael tried to help me in various ways, but I had nothing to look forward to. I called my daughter and son. They never called back. Michael went to see my daughter and son personally, and explain to them about all the lies their mother told them. They were not swayed and refused to talk to me.

Michael wanted me to see a shrink so I could learn to manage my emotions better and get some antidepressants. I kept wondering why he was going through all this excruciating pain for me. I didn't do anything for him and he was trying to rescue me from getting into this dark black hole. My own family, which I cherished for years and did everything for, was not with me. I guess life happens in unexplainable ways.

Weeks passed by. I was in this abyss of darkness and depression and was going even deeper. I had a dream and I saw Veronica bringing me a box that was full of roses and fragrance. The dream was so vivid that I could smell the roses in my room, even after I was awake. I got up and told Michael that I was going to America.

"Don't be foolish. I am sorry to say this, but you are suffering from depression and not in a condition to be in a strange place with people you don't know. You need someone close to you that can understand your emotions."

"But I have Veronica there and I want to see her."

"Do you even know if she wants to see you and what is happening in her life? She may be married by now and have kids. You will be more depressed over there and I can't let you do that."

But I insisted and he reluctantly agreed only if I could get in touch with her first.

I went to the American embassy and applied for a visa. I called her and left a message on her voicemail.

Then started the wait for her reply. It was like nothing I had experienced in my life. It was a strange feeling and I am unable to describe it completely in words. If you are or were ever in love and waited to hear from your lover or beloved, you will know. All of a sudden, I was in a state of bliss, and started feeling better. I felt like I could touch the sky. I wanted to leave Rome and see Veronica right now. I wanted to hold her in my arms and shower millions of kisses on her. I wanted to know her dreams and share my life with her.

When there was no reply for a day, I called her again and then again the next day. I wasn't going to give up. What if her number changed and I am leaving a message on someone else's voicemail? I had a sinking feeling in my heart. I thought my soul had found Veronica twice and then lost her. We tried to find her number from directory assistance and all other means possible, but were unsuccessful.

With no other way of knowing, I told Michael I was leaving for America. He resisted at first, but then, seeing my persistence and deteriorating condition, finally agreed.

Looking out the airplane window, I felt as if I was floating on the clouds. The cool breeze touched every part of my skin and I could feel her fingers caressing my hair. Every pore of my body, every cell was like a volcano spewing love out. I felt my heart come out of my chest and then it sat silently in my lap looking back at me. A strange euphoria took over every normal body function. I felt like dancing. I was in a strange zone of ecstasy and bliss. Why did everything look different and beautiful? Why does music fill the air while the whole Universe dances to the beautiful romantic tunes? Why do I feel that there is no pain or grief and everyone is happy?

Do you ever get that feeling? It must mean you are in love and you have a different way of looking at everything. Your perspective has changed. And everything is looking back at you differently. What a feeling! If you get these peak emotions and feelings in your life, seize them and cherish them in your heart forever, as you never know if you will get them again. I wish there was a way everyone can fall in love once even for few hours or days and feel it. I know our mind may think that love always leads to heartbreak, pain and suffering. But the feeling you get when you are in love is priceless and no amount of pain can take it away. Just open your heart, be vulnerable, leave the mind aside and let the love flow in. Take a risk and reach out to find your true love. Maybe it is not the right decision, but you will never know if you don't try. It could be the best decision of your life and leave you in bliss forever. You are meant to be loved. Just let the pure love flow through your body. Consciously choose love, don't get scared, immerse in the feeling, and drown yourself in the pool of love. It is the reason for your being. Everything else that you think is important really does not matter. The Universe will be on your side and will take care of everything. It will move forces of good towards you. Love will wash away all the past hurt, pain and suffering. You will sing and dance. A glow in your brightened eye will tell your tale of love.

That is how the Universe wants us to be, so when it sees that you are fulfilling its purpose, it will align with you for everything you require. It will become a coconspirator with you to create a fantastic dreamy reality for you. The Universe is all a blob of love, but it is unable to feel. So it created humans to feel the love through them. I lost a lot of material things when I fell in love with Veronica, but I didn't care. I realized that I didn't need them in the first place. When people say someone is crazy in love, they are right. But it is a different kind of crazy that gives you a feeling of euphoria without drugs or alcohol. You are high on life. You drink the elixir of immortality of love. You way of seeing the world changes completely. Noise becomes music, loss becomes another way to change your life, the breeze becomes cooler, beach waves comes to caress your feet like the soft hands of your beloved tingling your toes, the wind touches your face like your sweetheart's hairs, food tastes so good that it nourishes you from the inside out. There is no other emotion that will bring you closer to your life purpose.

I didn't know that before I fell in love with Veronica. I thought all that mushy stuff was for teenagers driven by hormones and had no real meaning to humans with a developed prefrontal cortex. But then I fell in love and realized how stupid I was. Just because we didn't experience something, doesn't mean it is not true. Just because you didn't find love yet, doesn't mean it is not out there waiting for you to align yourself with the greatest feeling in the world.

I took the cab from the airport and went directly to her home. Her sister Maria was there and told me that she had gone to Italy to see me. She didn't know where. I sat there, exhausted, thinking of where she was. What should I do? All of a sudden, it felt like all of my blood had been sucked from my body and I don't have any strength to even stand. My whole body started shaking with a strange pain that I had never felt before and I fell on the floor.

The next thing I knew, I was in the hospital and Veronica was right beside my bed. I suddenly felt much better and the doctors let me go home that night. I was diagnosed with extreme exhaustion.

Chapter 9

We sat on the patio sipping tea. The night was dark and loud with thunder and rain, but flashes of lightning illuminated Veronica. She wore white shorts and a light yellow blouse. She looked mesmerizing. A band of her hair kept falling to her face. She tucked it behind her ear again and again with a soft stroke of her fingers. Her white shorts morphed into light blue with every lightning strike. I could see her glowing as a marble in that flash of light. As if there were thousands of light bulbs emanating from inside out. Her whole body smelled like night blooming Jasmine. I would have thought she was wearing a fragrance that was intoxicating, but I knew she never wore perfume.

All this had a strange effect on me. I felt very aroused and wanted to make love to her. Momentarily, I felt so strong that I lifted her from the love seat and brought her into the open in the rain. Her breasts were swollen and she was all wet. I guess she must be feeling the same. As I put my hands on her neck, back and hips, she shivered and said something. I remember hearing, but didn't listen. She was the most beautiful woman in the world. What creates such a beauty? Our eyes or our thoughts, our brain or our heart? There is no way to describe that, as whoever goes through that experience will never be same again. It changes them forever and they cannot explain it rationally. Maybe it is not a rational phenomenon. Maybe it can only be felt by the heart and cannot be described in any language. There are no proper words to justify its impact.

Our wet hands touched each other. Fingers turned into a conduit to hearts with an electrifying effect on the whole body. As I touched her ears, she quivered under my touch and melted like a candle on fire. I felt my heart take over and morph my brain to engulf it in total love. I forgot that I was sick and dying. Suddenly we were completely naked. She was sitting on top of me. We were facing each other when I started running my fingers from the back of her neck to her spine. She looked at me with her glowing eyes full of life. Her upper lips lightly touched my lower lips. With her head turned left, she started kissing me. Our lips glued so tightly as if they never wanted to be separated ever. We started making love that was ecstatic. It was divine. Each and every cell of my body was emanating love. For the first time in my life I was afraid of dying. Heaven couldn't be better than this, so why leave this feeling of timelessness? It felt as if I was born again and starting my life. I felt like I was sixteen and had fallen in love with this irresistible girl in my school. I wanted to spend more time with her. Like I would get some incurable disease if I didn't get her.

Chapter 10

It was a month after we came to know about my terminal cancer. She walked into the cabin very excited. She was wearing a red shirt, black pants and long orange feather earrings. Her hair was tied up in a bun on top of her head. I don't think she liked wearing bras as I could always see the impressions of her nipples in her tops. She told me that it had not been the case before she met me. Now her nipples are always hard and her bras don't fit her anymore. "Nick, it must be a change in chemistry when I am with you." She told me that there is a Maharishi healer who lives deep inside the forests of Western India who can heal all kinds of terminal illnesses. She booked airline tickets for us to visit him. Doctors advised us not to travel that far as I may need to be hospitalized any time without notice. We didn't care about the doctor's advice and started packing to go to India.

We landed at Mumbai Airport after a long flight. It was 10 PM. We went through the immigration and moved to the baggage area waiting for our luggage. The luggage carousel started making funny sounds and passengers started picking up their bags as they came around the shining belt. We got our two bags and were waiting for the third that had most of Veronica's stuff. I had gone to a money exchange counter and converted some money. I also got some water from a vending machine and walked back to the baggage area where she was waiting nervously for her luggage. She bites her nails with her teeth when she is nervous and gets three horizontal lines on her forehead under stress. Her cheek dimples get deeper. She looked very cute and beautiful. I went and gave her a hug, but she was too concerned about her bag that she hardly paid any attention to me.

New bags stopped coming and her concern changed into a worry. We waited another thirty minutes. Everyone left with their luggage. We went to the Air India counter to inquire about our bag. They asked us to file a missing bag report, leave our contact information and told us that they will inform us as soon as they find her bag. Veronica was pissed off and not talking. I was just happy that I got to spend more time with her. No matter what happens, nothing can take away from the precious time we are going to spend together. I almost felt guilty that she had to deal with all this due to me. However my inner child who wants to have fun all the time took over and I shrugged the guilt away.

When you are with someone you love dearly, all the problems seem so small. What happens to those problems? Are they really something that should have worried us in the first place? I am not sure how being in love changes everything in your life. It opens up some hidden secret to happiness, the brain starts producing some strange chemicals that give you an exceptional perspective on everything. Atheists will start believing in God and their beloved looks and feels like the most beautiful person in the world.

Chapter 11

It was a very different experience than any other places I have visited as we walked out of the airport with our luggage. There were a lot of people making noise. It looked like they were arguing over something and were mad at each other. I realized that is what it looked like to us, but it is not true. That's how it feels when you don't understand the language.

There were so many cabbies jumping to take our luggage, almost attacking us. Veronica got anxious and scared at first. I, on the other hand, was enjoying the chaos. There is something about being so close to people that has a healing power. I could feel the calm in this chaos. A musty smell filled the atmosphere with a lot of humidity due to torrential rain. We hired a cab to take us to the hotel. He was a young man, with dark skin and a moustache, stray curly hairs, wearing a khaki shirt and pants. His badge hung from his left pocket. He whisked us through the crowd and pushed the luggage trolley for us to the taxi stand. Veronica was running after him, afraid that he would run away with our luggage. He had an umbrella that he gave her to protect her from rain, but it didn't do much for her. It was windy and the rain was so heavy that the umbrella kept flying away.

She looked so beautiful in her jeans running in the rain with completely drenched sneakers. Her thick black hair going wild in the wind and the rain. Her mascara spreading on her face made her look so wild and the anguish of having her baggage lost was rushing the blood to her beautiful face. I hugged her and tried kissing her right here in the rain, but she was in no mood right now. I think she was already planning ahead, thinking how to address her lost baggage problem. I have read and heard about monsoon season, but never realized how intense it is. We were not prepared for it at all. However, I enjoyed walking in the rain without a care in the world.

Finally we made it to the cab completely soaked. I unsuccessfully tried to talk to Veronica. This was the first time since we met that she ignored me and I was not feeling the love. Somehow worrying and overthinking kills the love and kicks us into a crisis mode.

I started a conversation with the cabbie on our way to the hotel.

"What is your name?" I asked him.

"Krishna, sir."

"How long have you been driving the taxi?"

"Almost six years. I came from my town to Bombay to become an actor around seven years ago. I still didn't give up on it. I know one day, I will be in the movies. I drive at night and look for acting jobs in the morning." He asked, "What are you here for, sir? Tourist?"

"Yes." I didn't want to bore him with details of my sickness.

"I can show you around the city in the morning," he said. He took out a crumbled card and wrote his phone number. I wasn't sure what plans Veronica had for tomorrow so I told him that I would call him if we are going to be in Bombay for more time.

We finally arrived with wet clothes. I gave Veronica my jacket to cover her now transparent wet blouse. You could clearly see her round firm breasts and beautiful brown areolas. I realized her habit of not wearing any bra needed to change as long as we are in India in this wet monsoon weather. She was clearly frustrated and exhausted from the trip. We checked in and the girl at the counter asked us if we need anything. Veronica frustratingly asked her if she had any dry clothes. She offered to send someone to the room and get her clothes, get them dried and return them to her in the morning when we wake up. We walked into the room, and the bellboy set down our bags.

I almost didn't want Veronica to change her clothes. She looked so beautiful with her wet tangled black hair with water droplets dripped on her breasts. The sight of her wet navel aroused me madly. I was so much in love. She seemed the most sensual woman in the world to me as she walked towards the bathroom to dry herself. Her style of walking always captivated and intrigued me. She walked like she was moving the mountains with her hips and her feet caressing the floor. I couldn't resist the temptation. I literally ran and hugged her from behind.

"Wait, wait…I am all wet and I don't want to make you sick," she said.

I was in no mood for conversation, too mesmerized by her beauty. I took off her wet blouse that was clinging to her body, freeing her breasts. She took a towel and started drying her hair with it. Her long neck stretched backward as she put her hair behind her head and knotted it with the towel. Her chest pointed outwards towards me, invitingly.

"You have to take off your jeans too so we can give it for washing," I said.

"Aren't you going to change your clothes? You didn't lose your bags," she said, questioning my attention as it was solely concentrated on her.

I opened my bag and took my pajamas out. I took off my shirt and pants. I realized my Calvin Klein underwear stood the test of monsoon season and was not wet at all. I contemplated my next move. She came closer to me and saw that I was completely aroused and ready to make love. She slowly turned around and took her jeans off. I was in awe looking at the dimples on her lower back right above her beautiful ass. I started thinking how lucky I was to have such a beautiful woman right next to me. She turned around with a wild look in her eyes and pounced on me like a cat and threw me on the bed. Her soft hands started moving all over my body. Her beautifully red manicured nails started slightly scratching my chest and moved down inspecting my whole body. I felt goose bumps all over me and felt I was going to explode. Her stiff bouncy breasts pressed hard on my chests and her slender legs wrapped around my one leg. Her hair brushed gently all over me.

She sat on me like that for minutes and we stared into each other's eyes with immense unforgettable love. I felt someone literally put a hot iron on my lap. She started whispering and making sexy sounds in my ear. I turned her around and before I knew it, we were immersed in love. It was sex enhanced by some unimaginable chemicals in the brain that made me start believing in the ultimate power of the Universe. That was our first sex in the land of mystics and Kama Sutra. I forgot I was sick. In fact in my whole trip in India, I didn't feel any sickness. I had more energy than I ever had in my life. Life was so beautiful. I was in total surrender to Love. I felt I had nothing to gain or lose, nowhere to go. Just totally immersed in the moment, I was exactly where I needed to be. My stars were aligned properly and I was in alignment with the Source.

I called the front desk and asked them to send someone to pick up her wet clothes left outside the door in laundry bag. We called room service, ordered some whisky and a chicken sandwich. We fed our tired bodies and slept in each other's arms.

I am not sure it was jet lag or the incredible sex that kept us sleeping till the following evening. Also I think you sleep better when you are sleeping with someone you love, all cuddled up and tangled. The comfort of that touch is healing in many ways and generates more love juices. I felt like we were on a honeymoon. No worries, no problems, just pure bliss! She was still sleeping, completely relaxed. Her eyes closed and her breasts moving up and down with her slow breathing. I didn't want to move and wake her up. I thought I was in a dream and I was afraid to wake up to let that dream go away.

Finally she woke up and we looked outside. It was still raining heavily. We sat on the covered balcony and stared outside at the beautiful Arabian Sea raging its full force. We didn't talk for an hour, as if our souls knew what we wanted to say. I never thought silence could be so comforting. The rain stopped abruptly and the sky cleared up. We could see the beautiful sunset far away on the horizon. I looked at Veronica. The golden light of the sunset falling on her beautiful relaxed body made her very attractive. Her curly hairs were kissing and caressing her voluptuous cheeks. As if she felt what I was feeling, she got up and sat on my lap with her head leaning on my left arm and legs hanging on the right side. She was wearing an orange top with low-cut and teal shorts. We stayed there cuddled for a while. I was unable to resist the sudden rush of blood in my whole body. We started kissing each other. I lifted her, brought her in the room and laid her on the bed so carefully as if she was a china doll and going to break. I started to advance towards her to take her shorts off. She resisted at first as she said softly that she was sore from last night. I understand as we had wild crazy sex last night, but I was unable to stop myself and continued slowly taking her shorts off.

She was already wet and I didn't have to make much effort to sink myself in between her slender legs, moving up slowly. She started responding with moans and held my head right over there very strongly. When I lifted my head, she was on fire. She grabbed me with incredible force and let me slide in easily in her moist, warm love. My whole body started feeling the joy of her love. I felt like my brain and whole body was going to explode. I turned her around and took her top off. I hugged her from the back, cupping her big breasts, and our lower bodies merged in juices of love. We became one and loved each other for a long time. Before we knew it, we both were fast asleep.

I was woken up by a big thumping noise on the door and fire alarms. We dressed quickly and ran out. There was an electric short circuit resulting in a fire and the firefighters started evacuating the hotel. We ran down the stairs and waited with other people outside the building. It was around midnight. We sat outside, Veronica being frustrated with the whole thing. We walked a little further from the hotel. I saw a few local couples walking, holding each other's hands in full moonlight. The dim light from the antique lamp posts were filtering through the trees and mixing with moonlight. I saw a guy with short pants strolling with a portable radio playing a loud Bollywood song. I was unable to understand the lyrics, but the song was very melodious. The light from the moon was reflecting on the waves of the sea and created a very romantic ambience. I was mesmerized by the magical moments that were provided to us by the Universe.

She looked so awesome with white light reflecting on her natural face and her hair completely soaked in moonlight. I needed nothing else for my spirit to be in this blissful state. However, Veronica really was not in a mood to walk as she was tired. We sat down on the corner on a big heart-shaped rock with waves from the sea touching and playing with our feet. What is it about this place that is making me so romantic? I felt like I was so much addicted and not satisfied with all the love that we made since we came here. I couldn't resist her full lips and beautiful eyes. I started kissing her. She let her hair down. It smelled like fresh roses and I was almost drowned in the intoxicating essence. She slowly leaned her head on my shoulder and let it rest there. I held her softly and we stayed like that for a long time. I could hear my heart thumping very fast as if it was trying to rhyme with the restless waves. I was totally immersed in the beauty of this place called Lover's Nest.

We finally realized it was late and started walking with our hands entwined. It felt like love flowed through our hands and passed through our bodies. An ice cream vendor walked by and asked if we wanted any. We had one ice cream on a stick and took our turns licking it. It was a thin condensed milk frozen on a stick. He called it Kulfi. It was the tastiest dessert I ever had. When we reached the hotel, they had the fire under control and were starting to let guests in. We went straight to bed in each other's arms and fell asleep immediately.

We woke up in the afternoon. It was raining heavily again. It feels like the sky bursts open during a monsoon. We started packing to take a night train to Ashram. I called the front desk for a taxi and they told me that all roads are flooded and closed. There are no trains running either. This time Veronica was not frustrated at all. She put on her orange and purple gown that should be classified more as lingerie than a gown. I had my pajamas on. We sat on the balcony on a lounge love seat made of jute with light green cushions. We called room service and ordered some tea and biscuits. Veronica put her head in my lap and almost fell asleep again with the soft touch of my fingers on her back and neck. Room service knocked on the door and I had to wake her up. She opened her sleepy eyes and gave me a confused look as if asking me why I woke her up from her beautiful dreams.

I had a small conversation with the guy who delivered tea and asked him when the rain will stop. He told me in a very unscientific way that sometimes it doesn't stop for weeks. I thought about checking the weather on TV and let him go. His answers were not what I wanted to hear anyway. The whole city stayed flooded with no buses, taxis or trains running.

We were stuck in the hotel for another three days. It started getting on her nerves, but I had no problems. I meditated two times a day, made love to the most beautiful girl and ate spicy Indian food. We sat for hours holding each other's hands. I lied down in her lap while she ran her soft fingers through my hair. Those days were the most beautiful days of my life. I knew I was sick, but it didn't feel like that anymore. I felt a new energy flowing through my body. We had gone to the bookstore downstairs and bought a copy of Kama Sutra—the ultimate sex guide. Every day, we read part of it and tried new ways of making love. We tried the most creative and intense sexual positions. Finally, the rain stopped and a beautiful sunrise greeted us from the windows. She was still sleeping, exhausted and sore from our long lovemaking adventures. The yellow rays from the sun filtered through the creases in the transparent white drapes and fell right on her face. Her mangled hairs and eternal beauty was enhanced manifold by this magical effect. She looked like a beautiful painting. I stared at her for a long time and then went down for a walk.

When I came back, she was still sleeping. I quietly walked to the balcony. I sat on the wicker chair dangling from a hook. I knew she was aware that I soon have to leave her and transition to another world. I will not be able to walk with her in her journey here. Why she is investing so much time and energy? It must be love. How is it possible that I didn't do anything for her and she loves me unconditionally? It must be that we are souls that were somehow lost in a past life and we are here to continue this journey.

Suddenly I felt a soft hand on my left shoulder and full, hard and plush breasts touching my right cheek. I was so much lost in my thoughts that I didn't realize when she came on the balcony and was standing right beside me. She hugged my head with both hands, her nipples touching my ears, and started kissing my head. We stayed in that position for a long time without saying a word. It felt as if there was nothing to say anymore. Everything was communicated from her heart to mine.

She sat in my lap almost dangling, with her arms around my neck. Her rosy lips kissing my chest, neck and cheeks. I moved my head slightly down and my lower lips locked with her sensual upper lips and we kissed so passionately until our lips started hurting with all the sucking. I wanted to live forever in this state, but I knew I had little time left. It wasn't the thought of dying that made me sad but the thought of leaving her. Quickly, I changed my state and tried to get out of it, but she sensed that something was not right.

"What is it, darling? Something is bothering you."

"Nothing," I said, trying to diffuse the thought.

"You've got to tell me," she insisted and got upset that I wasn't telling her my true feelings.

If there is one thing I did not want to see on this beautiful morning, it was her sad face. I wanted to be open and vulnerable with her.

"Why are you being so nice and loving with someone who is going to die soon? Don't you know it will leave you broken and miserable for a long time? You are intentionally setting yourself up for heartache. I am going to die soon and I don't want to go thinking I was selfish to get your love when I don't have much time left to give you back what you deserve." I started crying as I said those words. Just at that moment, I realized I had never cried in my life, not even in the worse crises. What is it that made me so open with my emotions and feelings?

"I know this cancer is not going to kill you. I have full faith that you will be completely cured," she said with conviction.

"That is complete bullshit!" I said. "It's a fucked up thought. You know that is not true. You have to be really stupid to believe that." I was actually mad and frustrated at myself for being so helpless.

She remained calm and replied without getting upset, "Maybe you don't believe in miracles and magic, but I do. Even if what you say is true and I only have few months to live with you, I will cherish them for the rest of my life. These few months of your love will be better than spending my life in some kind of a relationship where I don't feel any soul connection. When I am with you, time freezes and my body becomes formless. I feel like a marshmallow that is covered all around in hot chocolate of your melting love. My existence is changed just because I am in your arms listening to your throbbing heart. My scattered thoughts become very clear and I see you completely cured."

I stared at her and saw the divine love in her eyes. The same questions kept popping up in my head. How can you love someone that much? What creates such a feeling that we start declining the facts, start believing in magic and ready to fight the most ridiculous losing battles? What happens to all the fear that we hold so dearly and the logic that guides us in our life?

"Do you really love me, Nick?"

She didn't wait for me to answer that question. She didn't have to.

"Promise me today that for my sake, you will not bring thoughts of dying in your mind. You will spend rest of the time believing that you will be cured. That is the biggest gift you can give me."

And I promised her. Not that I believed it that day, but because she believed it so intensely that it was impossible for me to contradict. I started thinking that I will be cured and well.

That night, we boarded the train for Ashram. We fell asleep as soon as the train left Mumbai. I opened my eyes in the early morning and couldn't believe the sight from my window. The train was passing through a long stretch of green fields. The light from the full moon was spreading all over the fields. The crops in the farms were dancing in a rhythmic melody in the blueish white moonlight. There was a magic and calmness as if the Universe was showing me His best creation. The blue light from the moon lit Veronica's face, showing her best profile. I had enjoyed my journey from America to Ashram so far. I had the temptation to wake her so we could enjoy the beautiful scenery together, but I felt selfish doing that. After around an hour, the plains started changing into a range of mountains. The train passed through a bunch of small tunnels and the sun started to rise behind the mountains, giving glimpses of its golden rays.

Finally we reached our destination in the early morning. I woke up Veronica and got down from the train quickly. It was a very small station. In fact, it would be wrong to call it a train station. It was a small platform and a hut on the side of platform. It was made by probably cutting some big rocks in the mountains. We were surrounded by mountains all around. A taller mountain on one side with two waterfalls merging into a big stream at the bottom. The other side also had a mountain, but much smaller. We were the only ones to get down from the train. We were told that someone would come to take us from the station to Ashram. No one came. There were two railway employees in the hut that they called an office. We asked them how far Ashram was from the station. They told us it was couple of hours drive, but they don't have any cars in the village. Only the Ashram people have transportation.

We were hungry after the journey. We asked them if we could go somewhere in the village and get some breakfast. They told us the nearest village is an hour walk from the station. We didn't want to go that far as we had no idea when the Ashram people were going to come. There was a little vendor stall on the platform that served us tea, biscuits and some pakoras (salty fried chickpea flour snacks). We had no option but to eat there. He served us tea in very authentic clay pottery cups with the snacks. We told the station master that if someone from Ashram come, tell them to wait for us. He was very nice and told us that he will blow the station horn that we can hear very far. We left our luggage there and walked out of the station with our backpacks. We followed a trail leading to the top of the hill. Our eyes popped when we reached the top and looked on the other side. It was the most beautiful scene I ever saw created so eloquently by nature. It was a sensory overload unlike any other. My five senses were unable to grasp it completely. The unknown, unimaginable senses opened up to grasp the Whole. We saw sunshine reflecting on the two waterfalls and blinding our eyes. Water turned golden and came dancing down the falls like a beautiful Latina waist moving flawlessly on the Salsa floor. There were sounds of birds chirping, a nightingale singing somewhere with natural sounds of falling water adding to the whole experience. At the bottom of the fall was a big almost flat surface carved by falling water. The water then flowed in the form of a creek under a long railroad bridge towards our side.

We sat there on the top of the hill. I wanted to capture the incredible scene in my eyes and soul forever. We looked into each other's eyes without uttering a word, hugged and almost cried. We were so awestruck that time and space stood still for us. There were no boundaries to cross, no thoughts to worry about and nowhere to go, just pure joy in those moments. We walked down all the way under the falls, took off our clothes and stood there all wet hugging each other like a spiral. We were hugging so tight that there was no water flowing between our bodies, just outside our bodies as though we were one person and not two. If there is heaven, it can't be more beautiful and fulfilling than this.

It was afternoon now and we started getting a little worried about our ride to Ashram. We made our way back to the train station. When we almost reached the station, we saw an open Jeep pulling beside us. They figured we were the ones waiting for the ride and apologized for being late. Their Jeep had engine trouble on their way. They were two guys, one with a turban and the other with a big moustache and a hunting rifle. It made Veronica a little uncomfortable. When she asked them, they explained that we are going to pass through a very thick forest and wildlife sanctuary that is home to some giant squirrels, black panthers, jackals, monkeys, elephants, tigers and many more. They needed hunting rifles for protection. When Veronica signed up for the Ashram visit, she had no idea about the sanctuary. I was excited to know that, but Veronica seemed a little upset. She didn't say anything. I know that as she gets very quiet when she doesn't like something. She was probably upset for not knowing about this. They also brought some food for us. They grabbed our luggage from the station house and put it in the Jeep. After we were done eating, we hopped in the back seat of the Jeep. We passed through the thick forest along a bumpy dirt road that turned into muddy puddles. We sighted a tiger and a king cobra on our way. It started getting dark and they covered the Jeep with a transparent soft-top. We could hear the jungle was starting to get alive with various sounds.

Chapter 12

Shudhta Ring (Cleansing Circle)

Finally we made it to the Ashram gate. I couldn't fathom that there could be a place like this in the middle of a thick forest. We thought we were in an authentic luxury resort of some kind. There was a beautiful wooden gate and a sign reading "Baba Kadam Ashram." In the background we could see a beautiful range of mountains and streams, water falling from the mountains in the moonlit night. The place was out of this world.

Our driver dropped us off at the security gate. The security guard asked us some information and then he escorted us to a small hut made with bamboo and hay. A beautiful girl dressed in a white robe offered us some drink in a coconut shell, made us sign some papers and explained to us the conditions of living in Ashram. We had to be there for at least twenty-one days. We had to surrender all our belongings except for the clothes we were wearing. We can't have any contact with the outside world, can't take any pictures, etc. We will be provided the food, clothes and anything we need in Ashram. In return, we need to do Seva (volunteer work) based on our ability and talent.

After we were done with the paperwork, we were escorted by another girl to our little hut where we would stay for the first week. We had a closet full of clothes mostly white and saffron in color. We were told to change and put the clothes that we were wearing in a bag to be stored with our other belongings. There were no undergarments in the closet. When Veronica asked the girl about it, she said that we don't wear any in Ashram.

We were told that there are three phases of the retreat. In the first week we will be in the outer circle named Shudhtá where we will have to go through cleansing our mind and body. Then we will be moved to the middle circle named Yatra before we move to the innermost circle Adhyatma where we will be able to meet Baba Kadam for the final phase of our journey.

They told us to take rest and someone will come to explain all the other details. The cool breeze was blowing with moonlight as a backdrop. I felt very romantic. My body was on fire and I wanted to make love to Veronica. I didn't express it to her as she seemed to be tired when we walked into the outer gate of Ashram. Also, there were no doors to the hut. So I didn't feel comfortable bringing that thought to reality. I think the same thing was going on in her mind too. All of a sudden, inexplicably, all our tiredness was gone and we felt aroused.

Later, I realized it must have been the drinks made with herbs and ginger that gave us all the energy. We didn't care that there was no door. I hugged her from the back and grabbed her breasts and pulled her back towards me with intense passion. She unrobed herself and started making sensuous moves with her torso and hips gyrating uncontrollably. I took my robe off too. She threw me on the bed, grabbed me and merged with me so eloquently. With my face towards the door, I saw a woman who just walked in, to give us further instructions. I tried to tell Veronica, but she didn't care. The woman came back with more people. They watched us as we made love. Veronica screamed in pleasure multiple times during our sex, but no one spoke or whispered anything until we were done and my whole body was wet with her orgasmic fluids. It is impossible for me to describe in words how good I felt. It would be like trying to express the inexpressible.

They all welcomed us to the community. All of us walked on the other side of the outer ring for a moon ritual on the river. We were not allowed to ask other people any questions about who they are, how old are they, where they are from and what brings them here. We were told that knowing all those things about other community members will make us judge them and there is no place for judgment in Ashram. None of them looked ill, but neither did I. The ambience was so serene and peaceful that you feel healthy and good. It is impossible to think about sickness when you are surrounded by nature, peace and vibrant human beings. You can't think about darkness when the sun is so bright.

I didn't realize there were so many others here from all over the world. We went to a community kitchen where we were served vegetarian meals with a drink that was a combination of herbs with a yogurt base. Every vegetable was handpicked from the farm in Ashram. There were people among us with a very deep knowledge of herbs and mushrooms. They would go every morning into the jungle to gather special herbs for our food and drinks. The drinks were so intoxicating and relaxing. After dinner, we gathered in a big hall. There was a live band playing bizarre jungle music. They were beating the traditional Indian drums and singing something in their native language that I didn't understand. They were community members like us, who came to Ashram and never left. All of us started dancing to the music. I was surprised to see that almost everyone spoke English. I was told that Baba himself is a scholar and knows many languages including English.

Every day we got up and took shower. Then we go outside in this beautiful campus, do yoga, meditation, eat a most delicious breakfast, walk around on a different natural trail, come back, do Seva around Ashram, eat lunch, take a nap, get up and watch the sunset behind the river, then regroup in an open space lit with torches. They taught us how to make a bowl out of big green leaves. We put some ghee in the bowl and make a wick out of cotton to dip in the ghee and light it. We then let it float in the river while chanting Hindu mantras. They look so enchanting floating away from us illuminating the water. Some of us will make love outside under the starlit sky before heading into our own huts.

Chapter 13

Yatra Ring (Journey Ring)

After a week, we were moved into Yatra Ring, which means Journey. By now, we knew all the Ashram customs and each other. All of us became like a family. We were taught meditation and the practice of being quiet. We were told to think about what we are here for and ask the Universe to fulfill our dreams, desires and intentions. We are not supposed to doubt or think how it will be done. We were told to just let it go.

For the whole week, we meditated every day and set our intentions. I started realizing how the intentions started changing from the first day to the last day in this circle. It started with specific intentions and became more generalized as we meditated every day.

We were taught the essences of ancient Hindu scriptures from Vedas to Kama Sutra. We were asked to experiment with various teachings. We learned the art of meditation, of loving ourselves and others. We were explained teachings from many Indian books written by sages, on a wide variety of topics about how to heal ourselves externally and internally, how to perfume our body for exotic sex. They gave us specific instructions about how and where to touch our partners during different cycles of the moon for extreme sexual pleasure. We never had any idea that such writings existed and were written thousands of years ago. We learned that all that knowledge was true and practical.

With all this knowledge, we were totally transformed from doubtful individuals to the ones that believed in the Universe. We knew by the time we graduated from the Yatra ring that we are loved by the Divine. The Universe wants us happy all the time as we are an extension of the It. Our beliefs were slowly changing and we realized that we are all part of the Universe and are on the edge of an expanding Universe. The Universe or Divine or God, whatever you want to call it, feels love and joy through us as if we are senses of the Divine. We were ingrained with new beliefs that we are here to feel and express love in all its forms. That all things we consider bad are just our perceptions. The Divine is trying to prepare us for the ultimate super human being whose only intention is to receive and give Love, unconditionally. Maybe the incidents and the relations that we consider bad are just there to give us a perspective of what is so good in our life. How else will we know the good, great and the love if we don't have any idea about bad, petty and the hate?

The mystical knowledge about all the herbs and the plants, birds and animals, yoga and chakras was bestowed on us in amazing clarity with scientific explanations. I wondered how so few people know about this place.

At night, we will sit in Talking Circles around candles and talk about what we learned and what we are experiencing.

Afterwards, we perform special breathing rituals to have out-of-body experiences. I felt like I was in a trance in a Universe with fireworks happening all around me and then almost all nights ended with soft touches, cuddling and lovemaking with whoever is willing and accepting.

I woke up in the middle of the night from a strange dream. In my dream, I was in heaven and I was floating in zero gravity in a fog. It was as if I had an aerial view of what was happening. When I looked down, I saw beauty everywhere, beautiful lush gardens, mountains on one side and the ocean on another. People looked extremely beautiful and healthy, but a little weird. You could see inside of their bodies like an X-ray. All of them had very big hearts and very small brains. When they approached each other, their hearts vibrated rapidly and expanded to hug each other. They became one person and their hearts started beating together.

As I was fully awake, I decided to walk outside. The whole place was completely lit in moonlight. I started walking towards the fall. It was magical. I never saw anything more magical. I stood there for a long time. Time stood still. As I turned to my right, I saw something that I was unable to understand at first. It looked very beautiful, a moving mass of something. Damn it, I missed my glasses. I felt like I was on some hallucinogenic drugs and was unable to understand what was in front of me. I actually pinched myself to make sure I wasn't still dreaming. It looked like a strange animal and was moving in a rhythm. As I got closer, I realized it was two beautiful girls hugging each other so tightly that they looked like one. They were entangled like a braid with their hands raised above their heads, doing a weird dance and kissing each other under the fall. They were oblivious that I was even there. Then the girls lied on the rock and started massaging each other. It was the most loving act between two humans. They looked like fairies totally in love with each other. I watched them in awe for a long time and then walked back to my room, lied on the bed contemplating what I had seen. I started feeling like I was floating in fog. I was unaware that I fell asleep again.

Chapter 14

Adhyatma Ring (Spiritual Circle)

After a week each in the Shudhta and Yatra circles, I was feeling very healthy and peaceful in my body and soul. We hadn't seen Baba yet. People in the outer circles were not allowed to go into the inner circles. People in the inner circles were always visiting us guiding and preparing us for our ultimate innermost circle. Now we were moved into the final circle where we are going to be initiated and taught the ultimate lessons by Baba Kadam himself. Many of our thoughts and notions that were pre programmed into our subconscious were already cleared, our bodies cleansed by eating pure food and our sexual desires fulfilled by being with each other in a very intimate and passionate environment. I was given crushed herbs to mix in freshly squeezed pomegranate juice to cure my illness. I was not having any pains now. We were both excited and curious about how the Adhyatma circle was going to be. In fact we were unable to sleep the night before we were going to be moved up.

Then came our moving-up day. Everything looked different on that day. We woke up to a beautiful golden sun behind the mountains. Rays falling on the waterfalls made it look orange golden. The musical sounds of birds chirping created a magical effect on our minds. We were a total of twenty-five people—ten couples, two men and three young women in the ceremony. We were given new clothes, same colors as before, but with a little mustard-colored strip on the left sleeve. I realized that as we started moving from the outer to inner rings the robes were changing from very loose to getting tighter. They were still loose and comfortable. Other than the ceremony, moving was easy as there were no belongings to carry. We were just given a new place to live. It was different from the outer circle. In the outer circles we were living in small individual huts. In this place we were given beds in a big hall with no privacy. We all became good friends. I came to know that everyone who was there was not sick. Many of them were looking for peace, love and happiness. Only eight people out of twenty-five were there to cure some kind of an illness.

We were summoned into a big hall with a podium in the front. There were more than one hundred disciples in the hall. I was told that these disciples came into Baba's innermost circle and never left. We were told not to stand next to the person we came with, but to mingle with others instead. A beautiful woman named Ma Prema guided us into a meditation. She wore a golden robe tightly fitted around her breasts and waist. I have never seen anyone so beautiful, peaceful and blissful in my life. When she walked onto that podium, the room lit up with her presence. Her voice was soothing. It was like a dream. She was almost a goddess. She was Baba's right-hand person and very close to him.

After the meditation, we were given a break for drinks. The drinks were different than what we had before. We felt very relaxed after the drinks. We were told to gather back in the hall. There was soft music playing and a girl in her early twenties wearing a shining green dress was on the stage dancing slowly and smoothly with a beautiful rhythm. She asked all of us to start dancing. We were so trained in the other circles now that we followed her. Then the music started getting louder and faster. The dancing got faster too. This carried on for almost an hour when it turned into fast and loud drum beats and all of us danced in a frenzy. At the peak of the dancing experience, when we felt like our brains and hearts were going to explode, Baba Kadam walked up to the podium. He had a long beard, long hair combed back, his eyes glowing and I could feel an aura around him. He wore a shining blue velvet robe and a bunch of Malas (necklaces) with different kind of beads. His fingers had different kind of rings, and his forehead had sandalwood paste. Contrary to my expectation, he was very handsome, tall and muscular. He started dancing and clapping, following the crazy beats of drums. He was smiling the whole time.

We were told that he will call one or a few of the girls at random from the audience to give a demonstration of how we go beyond jealousy, possessiveness, ego and desire to enter a blissful state of love, surrender and non-attachment with a person or things. He closed his eyes and called the third girl from the left in row 18 to come up onto the stage. To my surprise, when the girl walked up to the podium, I realized it was Veronica.

Everyone was cheering for her, feeling somewhat jealous. She looked nervous and shaking. Baba hugged her and put his hand on her forehead. She was calm all of a sudden as if hypnotized. They brought in a long, wide bench with a plush red velvet cloth on it. Baba told her to lie on the bench and close her eyes. She followed his commands. Baba walked to the bench and sprinkled some golden dust in the air. All the lights were turned off in the hall. Everyone was quiet with a soft raga playing in the background. There was a red bright light on the podium over Baba and Veronica. Baba took off his outer blue robe. He wore a mini golden robe underneath. He slowly walked to Veronica, chanting some mantras, and started unbuttoning her robe from the top. After he unbuttoned her upper three buttons, her beautiful breasts popped out. He continued until the front of her robe was completely undone and dropped down on the sides of the bench. He asked her to turn around and completely removed her robe. He then started moving his hand without touching her body from her feet upwards to her thighs, butts, back and then to her head. He grabbed her head with both hands and turned her around slowly. There she was lying completely naked with her beautiful firm breasts heaving so heavily up and down. Her eyes were drowsy and she looked so beautiful.

Baba told her to shed all of her fears and inhibitions. He asked her how she felt and what she wanted. I was surprised to hear her say she wanted to have a wild, crazy sex. Baba asked her to pick anyone she wanted as her mate. I was so aroused and wanted to take her right away. I didn't care if so many people were watching. I thought obviously, she will pick me. To my surprise she said she will like to pick Baba. There was a sudden shock and silence among the audience. Everyone was stunned by her answer.

Baba was still smiling as if nothing surprises him. He asked her to proceed and fulfill her desire. He sat on the bench. Veronica took off his robe and started massaging him and playing with him. I felt strong emotions of jealousy and anger. I got very upset by her choice and actions. I felt so disconnected from her that I wanted to leave and go back home. How could she be so insensitive to my feelings? I felt that my cancer was an excuse for her to fulfill her sexual desires. It hurt my ego that she would pick Baba over me.

Although I was disgusted by the whole thing, I stayed. If I have to end my relationship with her, I need to know how far this whole ritual will go. But what happened with her being my sweetheart from a past life and all the feelings I have for her? Did I go through the same emotions in my last life? Maybe that's how I lost her that time.

My thoughts were interrupted by the soft moans I heard when she sat in his lap with her beautiful back towards the audience and her breasts up against Baba's face. Baba started running his fingers over her spine from top to bottom. She was very aroused and started moving her head in a frenzy. If she didn't come here with me, I would have thought it was pre planned and staged by Baba's crew. But I knew better, as we had no idea that it was going to be this way. We witnessed the very passionate sex. Baba had complete knowledge of Tantric sex and made Veronica scream with multiple orgasms. It continued for more than an hour. After, we were told to go back to our sleeping hall and rest. We all went back to our beds. Veronica dressed and came back to bed. I thought she would be so tired after all the things that happened on stage. After all, Baba is a strong man and took all of us by surprise. But she actually was very energetic and wanted more. I was overwhelmed with jealousy, anger and my hurt ego. I was in no mood to extend her fantasies to another level. I felt that I was just a tool for her and she is not in love with me. That's when I realized that everyone around us was very stimulated watching Baba and Veronica on stage. The hall was going through the experience of so much loving going around everyone. I was the only one not enjoying the bliss that was created after the ritual.

In the evening, we gathered in an open area with a podium in the front for a discourse by Baba. The sun was setting in the background beautifully. As it started getting dark, the whole place was lit by torches and Baba came up to the podium. So peaceful, calm, smiling, raising his hand to bless everyone. He then sat on a beautiful golden chair with red cushions and started with the chanting of OM, the ultimate sound of the Universe. Then he addressed his disciples and all of us who he calls his community.

"The Universe wants all of us to be Happy and Loved. It doesn't have any other agenda. Many of you will ask then, why there is lack, pain, sorrow, grief and sadness. Why do Happiness and Love keep on evading us? The reason is that we blocked the Universe from delivering us Happiness, Love and Abundance by erecting walls of Sex, Anger, Greed, Attachment and Ego!

"When sexual acts morphs into love, we awaken the divine power within us. When we learn how to forgive, anger disappears to bring us closer to our Source. When we learn to surrender and believe with full faith in the power of the Universe, our ego disappears. When we are aligned with the Source and practice non-attachment, we take away energy from the greed. We give the power to the Universe to provide us what is best. We become one with the Universe.

"Happiness and Love are the ultimate achievements of your life. They make our souls grow. Growth of the soul is the only thing we will carry when we complete our journey here. We are meant to spread that happiness all around us. When we get a glimpse of happiness, we ruin it by thinking it is not going to last forever and we don't deserve it. The moment we start thinking like that, we start moving towards the deep and dark trenches of sadness. The purpose of Life is to extend the love and happiness to everyone. We have to stop judging and love all that exists around us. Most of us know this, but refuse to believe and trust the ultimate power of the Universe. We are not supposed to just know about the divine powers, but experience it in our own hearts. We have to be a conduit for the Source to channel Love to all humanity.

"There was a reason to go through the sexual experience this morning. It teaches us to liberate from the rules of society that restrict us from doing what we want and be happy. It was meant to take you from the tribal mentality which tells us that if we Love someone, we can't express it openly as it shakes the basic pillars of the tribe.

"In the coming week, I want you to be mindful of every action. If you like a woman or a man, go and tell them. If you want to make love to someone who is not your partner, ask them and experience it with their permission. There should be no inhibitions, no judgment, no jealousy, and no commitment. These feelings keep us away from the bliss of the Universe that we are supposed to experience. Once you conquer and understand these negative emotions, you will know that all your problems will change into just experiences. These experiences will grow you to a point where you will know that everything is happening for a reason.

"In fact, ancient Indian temples have sculptures of couples having sex outside the temples suggesting that you can't reach the divine until you go beyond the routine. We should never have sex with anyone we don't love. We should only have sex with someone we want to and not with someone we have to. That will raise the act of sex to ultimate love which will bring us closer to the Source. If your partner tells you they don't want to have sex with you because they don't love you, you should be grateful to them as they spared you from committing a sin.

"Yes, it is a sin to turn a beautiful act of sex into a mundane task because you are chained by a relationship. Let them go without any anger or attachment. It should not hurt your ego. It is not personal. It is time for both of you to move on and experience something more beautiful.

"Anger, resentment and stress are the cause of all diseases. These emotions take us away from alignment with the Universe. Once you let them go, you will be healthy, cancers will vanish, and ulcers will disappear. The reason we keep holding on to each other in spite of hate, is that it hurts our Ego. This week, you will practice these principles and then you can leave whenever you think you can forgive everybody and love everyone. You will not cast judgment on any soul. You are not attached to the outcome of any of your actions. That doesn't mean you will not get excited about the outcome. Getting excited about the outcome will keep you doing things to manifest anything you desire. If you don't achieve the desired outcome, don't feel sad or depressed. The Universe may have a bigger, better and more beautiful plan for you. That is what a detachment from the outcome will bring to you. Think about the most beautiful partner you want in your life, the best healthy body or the greatest job. Write on a piece of paper everything you want, send that message to the Universe and then throw it away.

"Raise your energy and vibration level. Feel that the Source has started moving its gazillions of ions to prepare the best partner, job and health for you. You will be amazed what is delivered to you by the Universe. The Divine that created you knows how to deliver your best desires. You should have compassion for every soul on this planet as every one of us is a part of the same Divine love. We are not separate entities. We are all waves in the ocean, different, but part of the same ocean. We ultimately want to merge with the ocean and other waves. We want to take part in this dance with the Universe.

"Once you pass through the five blocks of Sex, Anger, Greed, Attachment and Ego, your every desire will be manifested in unimaginable ways. It may take some time for manifestation and sometimes you will be frustrated by the difficulties you encounter during the process of manifestation. Always remember, during those tough times, that it is growing you and preparing you to be ready for the wonderful desires you want to manifest. The Universe is waiting for you to explore your *gift* so you can spread it to the world. *It* wants you to become an extension of the Source to expand the consciousness."

For the next six days, every morning we meet in the hall, greet each other with hugs and kisses. We get together in groups, couples or alone in the beautiful sanctuary covering acres of the rainforest surrounding Ashram. We do not talk about anything except love. No conversations about how to pay our bills, our jobs, our family, nothing at all, is permitted or even desired by anyone, anymore. We go to the beautiful falls and openly make love to each other under running water, under the trees while rain pours on us, into the river stream.

I felt weird for the first few days just by the thought of Veronica having sex with someone else. I almost started thinking that someone is going to replace me in her life. I tried to have sex with others, but I wasn't up for it. I didn't feel any connection so I ended up moving alone in the forest for five days. On the sixth day, while on a trail, I saw a sign: "Do not cross – Private." As Baba told us to take risks and be open to possibilities, I ventured passed that sign. The trees were so thick they formed a canopy that no sunlight or rain could penetrate. I kept on moving. I don't remember how far I walked until all of a sudden I thought I was in a beautiful dream. I saw the side of a mountain with a water stream flowing into a lake. There were big rocks on both sides of the stream and on each side was lying two beautiful girls. They didn't look real to me. The girl on the left wore a shiny silver bra with her firm and well-rounded breasts almost fighting to be free, along with a long bluish green wavy skirt. The girl on the right wore some kind of a native Indian dress and a headband made with beautiful colored feathers. The sky was dark and cloudy. Then my head turned toward the lake and I saw a third girl who was so beautiful that I had to pinch myself to make sure it was not a dream. She stood in the middle of the lake with her head stretched back letting her long, beautiful black hair touch her butt. I could see her long stretched neck supporting a rounded chin. She was wearing a white sleeveless undershirt that was transparent and wet showing her bouncing breasts and nipples. I stood there behind the trees, entranced. The girls didn't have a care in the world and didn't notice me at all. I guess they were sure no one would come there. I saw lightning and black clouds start to open and almost instantaneously, it started raining heavily. The girl in the lake came out and walked to the other girls. Then they started walking away from me. I rushed to follow them to see where they live in this jungle.

After a short walk, I saw them going into a big hut. It was so big that it will be wrong to call it a hut, but it was a mansion constructed like a hut. They closed the door behind them, but all the windows were open. I was thinking of going back to Ashram, but the appeal of gazing at their beauty had a magnetic pull. I was curious to see what these beautiful girls are doing in the middle of nowhere. I went to one of the side windows and looked inside. I was surprised to see Baba sitting on a couch with his face towards the front windows. A girl naked from her waist upwards with a very voluptuous body sat on his lap with her legs over him. She had her back towards me. She wore a very colorful transparent piece of cloth on her waist tied with a beautiful deep blue ribbon. Her wild untamed hair was tied in a little knot on top of her head and then flowing down just above her waist. She had dimples on both sides of her spine. I noticed, from the back she looked so much like Veronica. If I didn't know that I left Veronica in the hall chatting with another guy in Ashram, I would have thought it was her. The similarities were so coincidental. I wish I could see how beautiful she was. The girl was massaging Baba not only with her hand, but with her whole body. Her breasts were rubbing on Baba's naked chest, going down on him slowly, but firmly. Baba sat with his eyes closed, relaxing almost in a meditative state and enjoying the whole experience.

He opened his eyes when the other girls walked in and addressed them very calmly, "You know, you are not supposed to go outside without guards. You have broken the rules of the house of pleasure. Get ready to be presented before the board in half an hour and you will be given a chance to redeem yourselves."

The girls obliged and went into another room.

Baba asked the masseuse to summon others in thirty minutes in the main room. He then walked to the back room. Something told me to go back to Ashram, but I stayed and moved around to the back of the house. Surprisingly, all windows were open. I guess they were sure no one would venture out that far in the jungle.

Chapter 15

From the window in the back of the hut, I was looking into a room, a big hall with a giant bed. The bed was round with no head. It was more like a cushion with red velvet cloth and golden wood lining all around it. There was a beautiful swing hanging from the ceiling on one side of the room. On both sides of the hall, there were stairs going up. There was one small room in the center of balcony opposite to where my window was. The front of the room was completely open. It was like a DJ booth in a dance club. The other three sides of the room had a balcony all around with beautiful sofa chairs. The room had a bench cushioned with lavender-colored velvet cloth.

While I was wondering if I should move to another window to see what is in the other rooms, I saw a woman with the three girls that I saw on the lake coming from the side and walked in front of my window towards the stairs. Their walk was very sensuous, rhythmic and sexy as if they are trying to seduce the gods to come and make love to them. They just knew the power they have in their sexuality and were expressing it through every pore of their bodies.

The girls were all wearing a lacy, knotted, free-flowing white cloth at their waist and golden, purple and deep blue small cloths knotted in a crisscross in the front to barely hold their breasts. The older woman was dressed in a saffron colored gown. She seemed in charge. She asked the other girls to go light up the room for the ceremony. They started lighting the torches that were anchored around the room on all pillars.

It grew dark outside, but the room was filled with warm, orange golden light from these torches. The girls then walked up the stairs where I couldn't see them anymore. The woman burned some kind of dry grass that filled the room with an intoxicating smoke. I am not sure how long I waited.

Suddenly the room was filled with Indian classical music with a soft vocal that was like a hymn. I saw twenty handsome young, well-built men walk in the room. They had no shirts on. They had pants with a colored sash, which were more like karate uniforms. In the balcony above the hall, Baba appeared with the three girls. They were asked if they plead guilty and ready to pay for it. The girls looked a little scared, but agreed hesitantly. Baba asked them to drink some potion from the bowls that were next to him on a small table and then lie on the bench in front of him. He then initiated the punishment by asking them to take off their tops and ran his hand softly over their bodies without actually touching. When they started moaning in ecstasy, he told them to go down by the pillars in the hall and surrender to the guests downstairs. He asked them to please the men individually and collectively in whatever way they want. The girls can't leave or take rest until the men are all satisfied. He said when you wake up and you are sore from all the activities tonight, you will remember that you are free to do anything here or outside the house, but you have to go with the guards.

The girls walked down the stairs with a combination of lust and fear in their eyes. They were topless, their naked breasts hard and nipples pointing upwards. Their transparent, free-flowing stripes sitting very low on their waists clearly showing that they are not wearing anything underneath. They walked to a pillar in each corner and stood there on one leg, bending another against the pillars. The men then came and tied their hands high with silken ribbons, touching them all over. I was very aroused by the whole experience. I didn't think it was possible, as I had very intense sex with Veronica, only a few hours ago. In fact, she was so sore and dry from all the lovemaking. I bet she is probably so tired that she is sleeping, giving her sore body much-needed rest.

Then all of a sudden, the music stopped and you could hear Baba in the hall speaking from the room's balcony.

"Gentlemen, I have a surprise for you before you get deeper in the night. I want five of you to volunteer to give up what you see in front of you. I want you to give up all the fun you are going to have with these three beautiful creations of the Divine and step into an unknown."

Five out of twenty men came forward.

"Baba, we trust you to lead us and we surrender to you all the pleasures," they said.

Once you surrender, you expand your field of receiving and more beautiful things start happening for you.

"Now I present to five of you, the most beautiful girl, who has learned and taught me the most pleasure giving Tantric sex techniques. She amazed me with the most awesome rituals. She asked me if she could watch this ceremony. When I explained that no non-participant is allowed to watch this, she agreed to be a part of the ceremony. Remember, unlike the other three girls, this is not a punishment to her, but a reward. So you five can't treat her like a slave. She will, in fact, will be the master and you have to be obliged by her needs. If anyone of you does not agree to this, you can go back to the other fifteen before I present her. She is not one of us. She is a guest at Ashram. So you can't see her face, unless she wants to show it to you. Do you agree?"

All five nodded their heads to agree.

Then in the Baba's room, on the balcony, an amazing girl stepped out. I think it was the same girl that I saw sitting so voluptuously and giving Baba the massage with her breasts when I saw her back in the first room. Her face was covered in a golden mask. She wore a golden cape opened all the way in the front, held together by a red collar around her neck. I, somehow, felt again it was Veronica. I so badly wanted to see her face. She came to Baba, stood up on the bench in front of him with her back towards us. She opened her hook at the collar and the whole cape fell down revealing her slender back and legs. She was completely naked except for the mask on her face. Looking at the beautiful natural dimples on her back confirmed that she was the same girl. It also reminded me again of the dimples Veronica had in the same place. She asked Baba to initiate her for the ceremony by infusing his Tantric energy in her. Baba picked up the bowl next to him, partially drank the white liquid and she drank the rest. He then brought her down from the bench. He picked up another bowl that contained saffron buttery cream with golden specks of glitter. He started rubbing it all over her in the front from the neck towards her bottom. When he was done, he asked the girl to sit on the bench with her back still facing us. She started applying the saffron cream to Baba. He stood there with his arms raised up and eyes closed, chanting some mantras. She then hugged him at the waist and started licking the cream from him. Her head moved in very smooth and soft motions and Baba's mantras starting to sound more like sexual sounds. Baba then lifted her with his hands, turned her around aggressively, cupping her big beautiful breasts and started squeezing them hard with her nipples in his two middle fingers. She started shaking her head in ecstasy. She moved her whole body and moaning. When she nearly reached the peak, Baba told her that her initiation is complete. She can go down now and participate in the ceremony. He said that he would be in the back room doing meditation if she chose to join him anytime with or without the five men.

At this point, she was so excited that she started to run downstairs. This is the first time I looked at her completely. If she was not Veronica, she was remarkably close to her. Her completely naked front was slippery, oily, saffron with shiny golden specks. A rush of weird negative thoughts ran through me. Now my Veronica, who I love so much, is going to pleasure all these strange men. I was feeling very aroused when she was with Baba. Now when I am almost sure that she is Veronica, the feeling of jealously and anger started taking over.

She walked to a man with a bony face standing in the middle of the five. She asked him to take her to the back room. He lifted her in his arms, kissed her on her nipples and carried her away. I couldn't see them anymore. I started feeling frustrated by imagining what they will be doing in the back room.

The other men in the room now started with the three girls. They made love to them standing near the pillars one by one. Then they moved them to the bed and asked them to be in all different positions that were not even described in Kama Sutra. When the girls had difficulty following their punishments, the other men lifted them and helped them to be perfectly positioned for the pleasure of the rest. When the girls grew tired, they were given a bowl of potion to drink for energy and continue. The other four men were watching this, sitting on swings on both sides.

Then I saw the girl with the mask coming out of the back room. The saffron cream from her breasts and her front was almost gone. She was glowing golden with all the sweat. She ran to the swings as if she didn't want to come out of the bliss she was in. She touched all the four men in the front in a naughty way, laughing. Then she said something to them and started running around the room with them chasing her. She started kissing the first two who were able to catch her and put their mouths on her nipples and took them to the inside room. She was having so much fun playing these games. It seemed from her expressions that she enjoyed it so much that nothing else mattered to her at this time.

Something shifted inside me. Soon all the negative emotions started to disappear. Initially it felt very awkward and weird when I saw her making love to someone else. Feelings of being rejected, cheated and inadequacy hurt my ego. Then it started to fade away. I realized that I should be happy if she is having a good time. It is not Love if we are not thrilled when our partner is happy and having fun. It doesn't matter if they are with or without us. We should cheer our partners on and wish them a lot of fun. That is what true love means.

The others continued. The girls seemed to be tired now and looked like they wanted to rest, but the men kept going. They were on the swing now doing so much kinky stuff and living out their fetish.

I saw the masked girl coming from the back with all three men with collars and leashes in her hand. Two of them were crawling and the third one was carrying her with her legs surrounding his waist. It looked like either they just finished making love or were still in the process. They came to the other two men and started taking their pants off. These two were so hard watching all the things happening around them. The guy that brought the girl tossed her to one of the guys. They started licking her all over. They were so excited that it was hard for them to wait. The girl got up, stopped them and signaled them to come inside. She could barely walk and was almost falling, from whatever they were doing in the inner room, but she was still jumping and screaming with joy. All five picked her straight up in a line and took her inside. I was so happy to see her having a wonderful time. I wondered if Baba was involved in their play or if it was just them. I felt no jealousy, no ego, no anger, and no frustration, just total unconditional love for her. I had a strong curiosity to go inside and see how they are playing with each other. But there was no way for me to see in the inner room.

I watched the people in the main hall. They had all three girls in the middle of the couch. They were clinging all around them and rubbing their tired bodies. It looked like the girls were just lying there passively and some guys still wanted more. They were all drinking that white potion and felt energized. I am not sure what was in that potion that made them so strong.

Then I saw the girl with the mask enter the hall, very bubbly. She wasn't completely naked this time. She had a pearl necklace and a green scarf running between her breasts, reaching her knees through the middle of her legs. She announced that she is there for anyone who will beg her and charm her. Then she sat on the swing and started swinging. The guys came and did various acts to please her. Some lifted her from the swing and made love to her, others chose to please her on the swing. They were all so excited to have her.

I wasn't sure how many hours passed. I felt so light, so happy that she was still having lot of fun. I started going back to Ashram. I saw in the sky the beautiful full moon showing me the way back. It probably took me more time to return as I was lost for a little while. I was so tired, looking forward to spread myself on my bed alone in the darkness. I threw away my clothes and without looking and slid under the sheets. It is only then, I realized, I wasn't alone. There was someone else in my bed. I felt her warm body next to me. I was so excited from the whole night that I hugged her from the back. She didn't say anything, but moaned like she was having a good dream. She was either in a deep sleep or pretended she was sleeping. I couldn't resist and started moving my hand all over her. She didn't resist and I started making love to her in the darkness without any fear or guilt. I knew Veronica would understand. Then she started moving and participating in the act of love.

After I had the wildest sex imaginable, I was shocked when she asked, "Where were you whole night, Nick?"

It was Veronica. I didn't say anything, but still wondered how she got there before me. Or was it really Veronica in the hut? I never asked as it doesn't matter anymore. I was free and liberated. That day when I sat for meditation, I realized those five men represented Sex, Anger, Greed, Attachment and Ego that I have to go past to reach my real love. As long as I am stuck in that, I will be blocking the energy that will flow naturally through my body to heal me.

On the seventh day, Baba called each of us in a separate room and gave us the Mantra. The Mantra was meant to remind us of the blissful feeling we had in our presence here. Whenever we feel any different in real life, we will close our eyes and repeat the Mantra to remind us of the experiences and the lesson learned.

Many of us stayed there for a couple of more weeks as the experience was so fulfilling that we didn't want to leave.

After thirty-three days, we left and went home. I didn't have any symptoms of sickness anymore. I felt wonderful. Still Veronica wanted me to go for a checkup. Doctors were surprised that the cancer was in remission and asked me to come back in four months for another checkup. Still no symptoms. I stopped taking medication. There was no reason to. We were so happy together. We lived and enjoyed every moment, every day, every month, every season. I often wonder, what cured my cancer? Was it the all the herbal potions they gave us to drink every day or the result of getting rid of negative emotions and stress? I guess I will never know. I also stopped questioning how and why things happen. I started concentrating on the experience and be happy all the time with love of my life.

It is six years since we came back from Ashram. I will go back every year. Doctors were amazed that my cancer was cured. I still don't have any signs of cancer.

I started my own business. Veronica quit her job and started helping me in the office. We were doing very well and were having a wonderful life full of love. I got so busy with work that I stopped all the practices of yoga and meditation taught to us in Ashram. I started thinking that I didn't need them anymore. The business stress built up and we started feeling the growing pains. We didn't have much time for ourselves. I was away on business trips all the time. I was getting stressed about how to bring the business to the next level and then suddenly, it happened.

I was on a business trip and I lost one of our biggest clients. I was stressed and I had a severe pain in my chest. I was rushed to the emergency room. They admitted me to the hospital. It was a heart attack. The doctors inserted a stent.

Veronica came and flew me back after I was discharged from the hospital.

I came home and rested for a couple of weeks. I started having pain all over my body. She took me to the hospital right away and they did more blood work. My cancer was out of remission. It came back. We didn't believe it at first. We got a second opinion and it was confirmed.

Nick's journal ended all of a sudden—either by the news of cancer or more likely that he wanted to live rest of his days completely immersed in total love and didn't want to waste time writing.

Chapter 16

Nick and I were sitting near the fireplace in the cabin. We rented this place after doctors told us that his cancer has entered the advanced stage and he may have only a few months to live. I was very frustrated, but he was calm and serene.

"How could you be so ignorant of the fact that you are going to die soon?" I asked.

"I am not ignorant, darling. On the contrary I am a happy and learned man. I know that I came to this world so I can learn to love, to feel that wonderful emotion that only lovers can feel and to smell flowers, to see different shades of clouds, to feel the sunshine and the wind. You brought me so much happiness that I am not afraid to die."

"But I am in love with you, Nick, and want to be with you as long as I can."

Very calmly, he said, "Being in love and loving someone are two different things and how do you know that you are in love with me? Maybe you just don't know and are trying to measure it by the tools and traditions you have at your disposal. If we are truly in love, then it doesn't matter if I live or move into another dimension, our souls will always be together."

"But I want to wake up with your physical body right next to me. I want to sit and sip hot cocoa with you on cold winter nights and have a snow fight. I want to swim with you in the clear blue ocean in summer and have margaritas on the beaches of the Caribbean Islands. I want to sit on the top of a mountain and admire the beauty of the foliage. I want to witness the spring bloom with you. I want to travel with you to the deepest jungles of the Amazon and I want to make love to you all the time. Nick, each cell of my body loves you so much. Why we can't be together forever? Who decides that you can move to another dimension and I have to stay here? Why, why, why?" I started yelling and crying with passion.

"Darling, we are all here to evolve our souls and learn life lessons. My soul's job is probably near completion and you still have to learn more lessons."

I realized that he never calls me by my name. When I asked him, his answer was that it does not matter what my name was as he loves my soul that is so beautifully wrapped in my body temple. He hugged me so intensely that my bones cracked. We talked for hours cuddling each other. He told me how when he landed in Rome after leaving America, he was arrested at the airport. His wife whose father was politically connected falsely implicated him for selling precious artifacts in America and that is why he couldn't come back to America sooner. She never told anyone including his daughter and son that he was in a coma after the accident. He told me how every atom of his being yearned to talk to me and be with me every single minute, every hour and every day in the prison. That I was the one thing that kept him going and he came to me as soon as he was out of prison.

"You must hate your ex-wife. She let you go through so much pain. According to your spiritual theory, what kind of a soul will do that?"

He replied, "I was very frustrated and angered at first. But then I started thinking about how you and I fell in love. All those feelings of anger and anguish had vanished. My heart was so full of love that there was no room left for hate. Darling, a heart can only hold one emotion at a time. If you have love in your heart, you will spread it all around you. Any negative feelings will automatically go away. My wife's soul was not bad. It was doing its purpose of guiding me to you and make me learn about true love. I don't have any bad feelings towards her. In fact, I am grateful to her for the path she has shown me."

Nick's physical state was getting worse every day, but he refused to go to the hospital, as he wanted to spend his last days with me. I asked Nick if I could tell his friend Michael to inform his children about his condition. He refused. He didn't want them to pity him and plan a mercy visit.

Then one day, Michael called and told us that Nick's son is getting married. Michael wanted Nick to come to Italy for the wedding and make up with his son. Nick wanted to go for his last effort to mend his relationship with his son, but the doctors didn't give him permission to travel. By this time, I was being selfish too and didn't want him to suffer emotional drama and face his wife and kids. He was very sad that he would be leaving this world without mending his relationships.

"When my kids were growing up, I promised them that I would write and deliver beautiful speeches for their weddings. I didn't get the chance to do it for my daughter. At least, let me do it for my son," Nick said. With tears in his eyes, he insisted that he go to his son's wedding.

He said, "I am dying anyway, darling. How much worse could it be? Maybe I will die a few weeks early, but I don't want to miss the joy of my son getting married to his high school sweetheart, Nicole. Nicole and I were very close from the time she first came to our home for my son's seventeenth birthday. They fell in love and were together since then."

Finally he convinced me to let him go. I told him that we will go together. We flew to Rome for his son's wedding. Michael was at the airport and noticed that Nick seemed weak and had lost lot of weight.

"It must be the healthy sushi Veronica is feeding you!" Michael said jokingly.

Nick brushed off his comment and started talking about the details of his son Pat's wedding. Nick wanted to see Pat and

Nicole before the ceremony. Michael invited both of them to his house for dinner next day at seven.

Nick was eagerly waiting to meet his son and hug him. He wanted to tell him how much he missed him. I had never seen Nick so exuberant and full of vigor before. He had a lot to share with his son after so many years. Then came the final rendezvous time, but they didn't come. We waited until nine and were very frustrated. Then we saw their car pull into the driveway. Nicole came out of the car alone. She came and told us that his son didn't want to see us.

"What happened? I thought he wanted to see me. How can he do this to me?" Nick was so upset that he started crying in agony.

Nicole said, "We were coming to see you, when his mom came. She asked Pat how he could go to meet his father after he abandoned his family for so many years for an American bimbo and has the audacity to bring that bitch with him, which clearly shows he is not remorseful at all. She created a lot of drama at home and told Pat that if we go to see his dad, she will never speak to us again. I realized early on that his mom is very good at emotional blackmail and Pat always falls into her trap. But I don't care and came to see my new dad. I love you very much and wish we could all be together."

Nick started murmuring and become very incoherent. I got scared. Then he got into a state as if he was not even with us and started telling Nicole his true story. "I hope you will tell that to my grandkids and explain to them their grandpa wasn't as bad as he is projected to be. He was just victim of lies perpetrated against him."

"I don't want you to be sad, Dad. I will tell everything to your son first," Nicole said.

Nick and Michael both knew that would not have any effect on Pat. Michael tried that earlier with no effect on him. I wanted to go back to America, but Nick wanted to stay until the wedding day. I think he was hoping that some miracle will happen and that his son will come to see him and invite him to his wedding. But as expected, no miracle happened, no one came and we flew back to America with heavy hearts. Nick was so quiet. I felt like I was traveling with a ghost.

Chapter 17

It went on for weeks. One day, Nick completely shifted. He woke up all happy and cheerful. I knew his end was near, but he was in such good spirits.

It was raining heavily. I could feel the wetness in the air, hear the thunder and see the lightning. We were sitting on the loveseat in the patio drinking tea. Nick looked very handsome in pajamas. I bought those for him because light green looks so good on him. It must have been the rain that made me feel very sexy and terribly attracted to him. I didn't express those thoughts to him. By some magic, he read those thoughts and came closer to me. He started touching my hair and I felt his fingers' hypnotic effect on me. I felt insane love taking over. I didn't want to go any further as I knew he was sick and making love may be frustrating to his weak physical state. How do I let him know that I am deeply in love with him? We as normal human beings don't have many other ways of expressing love other than sex. I felt he knew somehow what I was thinking and I felt naked. He started touching my ears and face with his fingertips. I was going to melt under his soft touch. He lifted me from the seat and brought me out of the patio in the pouring rain. The sound of rain falling on small trees and wind blowing over small leaves in the lake house provided a mesmerizing backdrop. It was if the whole Universe colluded to provide us with a perfect atmosphere for an eternal love.

I was afraid of going in the rain. I catch cold very quickly. I didn't want to be sick and affect his already weakened immune system, but it didn't matter anymore. Those subconscious thoughts were eliminated immediately and my conscious state that wanted only my wishes and desires to be fulfilled took over. I was completely wet inside out with water creeping underneath my white cotton pants. My wet white shirt was almost transparent now. My breasts were trying to break all my shirt buttons. My pants felt smooth like silk and every part of my body radiated with love. He touched my breasts and back of my neck, back and hips with his fingers. I couldn't hold myself together. I melted in his arms like a candle—smooth, hot, wet and shapeless. The mind became clear like a crystal with no physical boundaries at all. Our bodies became one in that blissful state.

We made love that felt out of this world. The rain and thunder stopped suddenly. The moon came out from behind the clouds. Moonlight lit the whole front yard and his face looked so beautiful. It was magical. We spent the rest of the night looking at each other relaxing on the patio, but didn't speak a single word. I guess there was nothing to be said, as our hearts spoke with each other so openly and truly. I never believed in God, but in those moments, I felt I was much closer to accepting His existence. I never thought we could experience His power making love. It was meditation at its best and I wanted to hold onto that feeling. During the orgasmic state of love, you are at the top of world and imagine if you can create that feeling whenever you want. I guess that's what Buddha must have felt during his meditation and he never came out of that state. Just orgasmic—all the time, on demand.

We deeply enjoyed his last few weeks. We listened to music, we sang, we danced, we gazed at the stars, we hugged, we laughed, we cried, we walked through the woods, we touched the wind, felt the raindrops on our heads and dew drops on our bare feet, we listened to the chirping of the birds and silence of the nights and we made love in sultry nights. I wonder how a person so weak with sickness can make love that is almost mystical. I guess we will never know the answers to the infinite love he had for me. The love that is all around us. We just have to recognize it, feel it and embrace it. You may find it in the strangest of places. Get out of stereotypical thinking about love and connect with your heart. If you like someone, express it; if you love someone, show it. Don't worry about how bad it will look if it doesn't work out. Just follow your heart and find your love. You will know how the power of love can heal your soul in mysterious ways. You will find extreme happiness even if it gives you heartache in the end. Capture that feeling and remember how good it felt to be in love.

<h1 align="center">Chapter 18</h1>

Nick looked very happy, healthy and full of exuberance today. He got up early and made my favorite breakfast: sunny-side eggs, bacon and buttered toast with exotic tea with lime and honey. He didn't eat breakfast with me today.

I asked, "Why aren't you eating?"

"You made breakfast for me many days, darling, today it is my turn. I want to watch you eat. I want to enjoy and cherish this moment for rest of my life. Oops… I am sorry, I don't have any life left. I am not afraid of dying, but I am afraid of losing you again. I don't know how many times I have to reincarnate so we can spend most of our life together and not just a few days, weeks or months."

I thought he was getting extremely emotional and wanted to break the pattern. We were running out of household stuff and needed to fill his prescription.

"Nick, I am going to town to run errands, get groceries and your prescription. Do you want anything special?"

"I don't need anything. Please don't go now."

"You look great today, I don't think you need a babysitter today and you need your medication," I said laughing, trying to lighten the mood.

It was a nice sunny day. I sat with him for a few hours in the lounge chair in the back yard. He just stared at me the whole time. His hypnotic blue eyes were so deep and clear, I felt I was going to drown in that ocean of love.

Finally I told him that I will be back from town in two hours after a quick run. He didn't say anything and looked at me in a way that was unfamiliar to me. I didn't know what his eyes were trying to say.

I came back after a couple of hours. He was sleeping in the lounge chair in the back yard. The golden light of sunset was glowing on his face. I didn't want to disturb his peaceful nap. I went to the kitchen and started preparing his favorite Chicken Marsala and spaghetti. And of course, he loved mashed potatoes with gravy. We had such a wonderful day and I wanted him to have a great night too. It was getting darker and dinner was ready.

I walked outside and called him for dinner. I finished setting the table and he didn't come in. I thought he didn't hear me as he will always jump when I announce that I made Chicken Marsala. I went outside and almost screamed his name. He didn't move at all. I got scared and ran to him. I tried to wake him, but was unsuccessful. He wasn't breathing. I called the ambulance, but he was gone long before that.

Blanket you used is still unfolded

Tea Cup still has your lovely mark

Your love is still on my white clothes

Towel you used is hanging in the dark

Your slippers, your pajamas, your red scarf

Why didn't you take everything away

My memories, my breath and my eyes that bleed

When you took my heart and left me to grieve

He was right—there was no one beside him, not even me. So if he was right about that, there is a good chance he will be right that he will find me again. I wasn't sure how this works. How is he going to recognize me in his next life? But I started believing what he said.

So long, Nick, with your infinite Love and finite life. May we meet again and continue our journey of Love.

www.ingramcontent.com/pod-product-compliance
Lightning Source LLC
Chambersburg PA
CBHW070329120726
47909CB00008B/2652